ALMOST SISTERS

THE SISTERS TEAM

KATHRYN MAKRIS is the author of a number of books for young adults, some of which have been translated into Spanish, Italian, French, and German. She also works as a reporter and has published articles in *Mother Jones* magazine, the San Francisco *Chronicle,* and other publications. Her interview credits include the Reverend Jesse Jackson, Ralph Nader, Gloria Steinem, Sissy Spacek, Ted Danson, "Colonel" Sanders, and Benji the dog. The ALMOST SISTERS trilogy are her first books for middle grade readers.

She enjoys hiking, swimming, nature study, and travel, migrating regularly between California and the state she grew up in, Texas.

ALMOST SISTERS
THE SISTERS TEAM

KATHRYN MAKRIS

AN AVON  CAMELOT BOOK

This book is dedicated to Dr. B., Mrs. B., and L.B., with deep gratitude for their love and for their roles in producing my best friend.

For much helpful information, thanks to Corporal Susan Green, California State Humane Officer (who also saved my dog's life!), to wildlife expert Sandi Stadler, and to schoolteacher John Isberg.

THE SISTERS TEAM is an original publication of Avon Books. This work has never before appeared in book form.

AVON BOOKS
A division of
The Hearst Corporation
1350 Avenue of the Americas
New York, New York 10019

Copyright © 1992 by Kathryn Makris
Published by arrangement with the author
Library of Congress Catalog Card Number: 91-92035
ISBN: 0-380-76056-8
RL: 5.1

First Avon Camelot Printing: January 1992

CAMELOT TRADEMARK REG. U.S. PAT. OFF. AND IN OTHER COUNTRIES, MARCA REGISTRADA, HECHO EN U.S.A.

Printed in the U.S.A.

OPM   10 9 8 7 6 5 4

Chapter 1

"This is scary," said Vanessa Shepherd. She had just left her house with her best friend and stepsister, Ricki Romero. Along with their dog, Kirby, they were walking down the street to see Clementine Hewitt.

"Clementine Hewitt," said Ricki, tossing a long black braid over her shoulder, "is scary."

Vanessa fanned the hem of her green T-shirt in and out and blew upward at her custard blond bangs. It was late August, a week before the start of school, and hot. "Maybe we're wrong," she said. "Maybe the spooky person glaring at us from her window that day wasn't actually Clementine. It could have been a visitor."

"Great." Ricki twisted her cinnamon brown face into a grimace. "With visitors like that, who needs Freddy Krueger?"

"Oh, Ricki, hush. You're scaring me worse." Vanessa held tighter to Kirby's leash. "We *have* to talk to Clementine. For one thing, we have to return these love letters to her." She patted the stack of envelopes in her back jeans' pocket.

1

"We do? I don't think we do." Ricki bunched her mouth to the side. "They were in your closet, after all, Vee. I mean, she moved out and left them there. I think we should at least get to read them."

Vanessa pursed her lips. "We've been through this a zillion times, Ricki. We aren't reading the letters. They're Clementine Hewitt's. And *I* found them."

Ricki sighed. "All right, all right. Be that way."

"Anyway," Vanessa went on, "your mother and my father will never let us live it down if we don't go talk to Clementine. You've heard them teasing us about being the Sister Sleuths and Sisters Team and ghostbusters and everything. We have to ask her what to do about the raccoons in our attic."

"How about the bats in her belfry?" asked Ricki.

Vanessa giggled. "Do you really think she's nutso?"

Ricki shrugged. "Dr. Rosen said she never goes out. She spends all her time taking care of sick wild animals. But hey, I thought you weren't scared of anything with Kirby around. I thought this big black walking rug was supposed to protect us."

"He does," maintained Vanessa. "He will." She gave Kirby a little scratch on his large, shaggy head, which stood almost as high as her chest.

Over the summer Vanessa had grown from four-foot-ten and three quarters to four-foot-eleven and a half, but in the last month Kirby had grown, too. Now he weighed one hundred and two pounds and even made tall, leggy Ricki look petite.

"Anyway," Ricki said, "I bet that white-haired person in the window *was* her. Remember what

2

Dr. Rosen said? That we should 'approach her with extreme courtesy'? Clementine's a loner, and she—''

"Oh, look!" interrupted Vanessa as they passed the ivy-covered stone house next door to theirs. "There's Dr. Rosen in his front yard. Hi, Dr. Rosen!"

The round, balding man looked up from a hedge bush he'd been staring at. Ricki saw a puff of smoke rise from his pipe to cloud his face. He lifted a hand in a slow-motion wave at the girls, then slowly looked back down at the bush.

"We have weird neighbors," whispered Ricki.

"Dr. Rosen is just eccentric. Being a retired chemistry professor and all. Maybe Clementine is like that, too. Just eccentric. You know, different."

"Kind of like Great Aunt Allegra?" asked Ricki.

Vanessa smiled, thinking of her father's eighty-year-old aunt, who had stayed with them after Ricki's mother and Vanessa's father got married in June. "Clementine probably even believes in ghosts, too, like Aunt Allegra does."

"Well, I guess she probably does. I mean, Clementine and her family moved out of our house years ago, because they thought the raccoon noises were made by a ghost. The ghost of her ex-boyfriend, a sailor who died at sea!" Ricki snickered.

Vanessa nodded. "And he came to haunt them, because she got engaged to someone else! Isn't that a creepy story? Even *we* believed it at first."

"That was 'cause your Aunt Allegra convinced us. The whole time our parents were gone on their honeymoon she told us ghost stories."

3

"Well, she's *your* aunt, too, Ricki. Share and—"

"Share alike. I know. Now that we're sisters." Ricki grinned, black eyes sparkling.

The girls gave each other high-five congratulations slaps. The Sisters Scheme had worked. With a little matchmaking, the two of them had gotten Ricki's widowed mother and Vanessa's divorced father to marry. Kirby joined in with an excited bark, then gave Ricki's open palm a huge slurp.

"Yuck." Ricki made a face and wiped the hand on the seat of her denim cutoffs. "Why doesn't he ever do that to *you*?"

"He wants to show he likes you. He knows I know he likes me," explained Vanessa.

Ricki sighed. She hadn't been a big fan of dogs. Gradually, though, she was growing used to being a part of this one's family. Share and share alike.

"Oh, look, Ricki," said Vanessa when they reached the corner. "This was where we found him."

"Who?"

"Kirby. Right here by—" Vanessa lowered her voice. "By Clementine Hewitt's house."

"Hah! He found *us*, you mean. And nearly scared me to death. We were looking down the hill at the spooky-looking person in Clementine's window, and he sneaked up from behind and slurped my hand." Ricki made a face at Kirby. Then she asked, "Well, are we going to do it, or aren't we?"

"Do what?" Vanessa frowned through the thicket of oak trees at Clementine's brown house.

"Talk to her! Let's get it over with. I want to get

back home and practice my softball pitch. My last game is this week. You can catch for me."

"I don't think so."

"Oh, come on, Vee. It won't kill you. You need the exercise. We start junior high next Tuesday, and they've got P.E. in junior high. Physical Education," Ricki teased her sister.

Vanessa's chest squeezed tight. The mere mention of junior high made her feel even more nervous than the thought of talking to Clementine Hewitt.

"You're pale and skinny, Vee," Ricki went on. "We've got to give you some muscles. See, look at mine." Ricki flexed her glossy brown arm and brought a long, toned leg up in a sweeping arc. "Sports keep you in shape."

Vanessa sighed. "Fine. You can be the jock in the family. I'll never get a tan or muscles, no matter what."

"They'll make you get muscles in P.E. You *have* to exercise."

"Do we have to talk about it now?" Vanessa nibbled nervously on the inside of her cheek.

"For cripes sake, Vee, it's only school." Ricki rolled her eyes. Vanessa acted as if junior high were the end of the world. The idea of meeting loads of new people made her antsy. Vanessa sure could be shy. Personally, Ricki couldn't wait. It was so exciting! Right now she and Vanessa were only twelve years old, but after the end of their first year in junior high, they'd be teenagers!

They rounded the corner to Cerrito Avenue, look-

5

ing for Clementine's driveway. They finally found it—steep, cracked, and weedy.

"I wish I had brought my camera," said Ricki. "This place is so spooky, it would make really great pictures."

Vanessa shook her head. "I wouldn't want to wait around while you took pictures here."

In a few minutes the girls stood at the front door, surrounded by a jungle of overgrown bushes and vines.

"Remember the cages that used to be out here?" whispered Vanessa. "They're gone. Maybe she moved them. I guess they were for the injured animals."

"Or maybe for children who come and knock on her—"

At that moment the door flew open and banged hard against the wall. Ricki, Vanessa, and even Kirby jumped back and squealed. The door continued to bang, over and over. Huddling together, Vanessa and Ricki peered into the long hall beyond. It was dark and empty. There was no one there.

Then, suddenly, there was. A crazy-looking person with wild white hair, glaring at them. "Get that *dog* out of here!"

Her voice was deep and raspy. Small eyes squinted angrily above a long, bony nose and an enormous mouth painted bright red. The mouth opened again to reveal yellow teeth. "Go! Now! I said, git!"

"But—" Vanessa began.

Ricki tugged on her arm. "Let's go!"

Kirby barked.

6

"Kirby, quiet," said Vanessa. "Sit."

Kirby looked up at her, whining.

"Quiet, Kirby. Sit," Vanessa repeated.

Kirby sat.

"I told you to get that dog off my property!" the woman commanded. Her hair stuck out in all directions, as if she hadn't combed it in a month. What she wore looked more like a gray sack than a dress—baggy and missing buttons.

"Come on, Vee!" Ricki whispered, still pulling on her sister's arm.

Vanessa tugged back. Kirby whined again.

"But, Miss Hewitt," Vanessa began again. "We just want to—"

"How'd you know my name?" the voice rasped, low and threatening.

Ricki's eyes widened to the size of quarters.

Vanessa finally managed to shake Ricki's hand off her arm. "Well, our next-door neighbor, Dr. Rosen, said—"

"Rosen? Lenny Rosen? That milquetoast sap? What does he want?"

"No. Not him. I mean— I mean, he doesn't want anything," Vanessa stammered.

"But *we* do," Ricki finally managed to put in.

"Dr. Rosen said you know about animals," said Vanessa quietly.

"What animals? What do you want?"

"Raccoons," Ricki managed to say. "We have some in our attic."

"So? What are you pestering me for? Get going!"

"But he said you could help us get them out and take care of them," Vanessa persisted.

"Call the animal shelter," said Clementine. "And get off my land with that fleabag."

Ricki saw Vanessa's back stiffen.

"Fleabag?" Vanessa repeated, pursing her lips.

"That's what I said," confirmed Clementine. "I'll call the animal shelter myself if I ever see that mongrel here again. Do you hear me?"

Ricki bit her lip. Whenever Vanessa's chin thrust out the way it was doing now, it meant trouble.

"Kirby," said Vanessa, with one hand on his head and the other on her hip, "is a wonderful dog. You can't talk about him that way."

Clementine's eyes squinted even harder, so that Ricki could barely make them out in the fleshy folds of her face. Then the smallest trace of a smile pulled at Clementine's heavy red lips, making her teeth show through in a snaky yellow line. "Oh, I can't, can't I? Hmph. You just go on now. Go!"

Ricki whispered, "Vee!"

Vanessa's chin still stuck out. "Well, thanks *so* much for your help, Miss Hewitt. By the way, these are yours." She pulled the envelopes out of her pocket and handed them to the old woman. Then she spun on a heel and marched up the driveway, as if it was just what she'd intended to do all along.

Ricki and Kirby rushed to follow.

The door slammed behind them, hard.

Chapter 2

"I still can't get over how rude she was to us."

Kirby opened one big brown eye to look at Vanessa from his favorite spot on her bedside rug.

"Imagine, calling you a fleabag! How dare she?" Vanessa muttered as she pulled her yellow T-shirt off over her head. She folded it back into a dresser drawer and pulled out a pink one.

It was Tuesday morning, the first day of junior high. Vanessa was trying very hard not to think about that fact. Thinking about Clementine Hewitt's rudeness was a lot less disturbing.

Still, her nervousness about junior high wouldn't go away. Neither would the problem of what to wear. Maybe T-shirts were too casual.

She caught a glimpse of herself in the mirror. Taking off the shirt had mussed her bangs and skewed her silver barrette. "I'll never be ready in time!"

In her closet she found a red checked blouse with buttons shaped like ladybugs. After slipping it on, buttoning the bugs, and tucking it into her new blue jeans, Vanessa frowned at herself. "Now I look like a picnic blanket."

9

Kirby rested his black shaggy head on his giant paws and sighed.

"The first day of junior high!" Vanessa reminded him, chewing on the inside of her cheek.

She could hardly breathe. Her chest felt squeezed by nervousness. Maybe it would move to her stomach, where it would become a stomachache, and then she could stay home.

"You in there?" called Ricki from the hall.

In Ricki shuffled, with long, sleep-fuzzed braids. One brown-skinned fist rubbed her eyes, while the other reached toward the ceiling in a lazy stretch.

Kirby's tail thumped a loud hello.

"You're just getting up?" Vanessa's eyebrows arched high.

Ricki nodded. "Yup."

"It's seven-fourteen! We're going to be late!" Vanessa blinked at her green plastic wristwatch.

Ricki yawned. She flopped down on Vanessa's bed, long legs and arms trailing limply over the sides.

Kirby gave her palm a wet slurp.

"Yuck," said Ricki.

As usual, Kirby seemed to think that meant, "Gee, thanks," so he gave her other palm a slurp.

"Ricki, go get ready!" Vanessa planted a hand on her hip. "We have to leave in thirty-six minutes!"

Another yawn. "How come school starts so early this year? We didn't have to be at Kennedy until eight-thirty."

During four years of being best friends, Vanessa thought she should have gotten used to Ricki's relaxed attitude. But sometimes she wondered how

10

the two of them even got along, being so different. And how on earth did they actually manage to have fun together?

"We're not at Kennedy Intermediate anymore, Ricki. This is *junior high*," Vanessa pointed out. "Aren't you just the smallest, tiniest bit, well, nervous or anything?"

"Nervous?" A shrug. "I guess so."

Vanessa sighed.

Ricki yawned again. "Hey, I was wondering, when are the animal shelter folks coming to get the raccoons?"

"They told Dad some time this week. First they want us to be sure that the dirty socks and radio tricks aren't working."

"I guarantee they're not." Ricki shook her head. "I heard the raccoons last night, loud and clear. Sounded like screaming. Maybe the mom likes the smell of our dirty socks and the sound of rock music blasting out at her all day."

"She's not supposed to," said Vanessa. "The officers told Dad on the phone that she would hate it. They said if we put some used socks in the attic and played a radio up there really loud, the mother would want to pick up her babies and take them somewhere else."

"Not *our* mama raccoon. Ours must be a rock 'n' roller. She's gotten to like it because of hearing your dad's band practice all the time." Ricki gave another stretch and snuggled into Vanessa's pillows.

"Ricki, *please* go get ready."

11

Ricki scratched her ear, then got up. "Okay, okay." Vanessa could get so uptight about things!

Minutes later, wearing her Oakland A's baseball T-shirt, cap, and oldest jeans, Ricki strolled into the kitchen. Anita, her mother, leaned against the sink holding a coffee mug and the newspaper. Her mom's job as a financial advisor meant she got to tell people what to do with their money, so she read *The Wall Street Journal* front page to back every morning. Vanessa's father, Andy, stood at the stove flipping a pancake. Vanessa sat at the table, frowning at Ricki.

"You're wearing *that*?" she asked.

Ricki rolled her eyes. "It's only school, Vee."

"Is there a dress code at Roosevelt?" Anita asked, peering at Ricki over the tops of her reading glasses.

Andy shook his head. "Not in the student handbook the school sent. At least, nothing that would outlaw trusty ol' jeans and T-shirts. But if Ricki were to grow a beard——" He stroked his own short, brown one. "Now *that* would be a problem."

"I see," said Anita. Her dark brown eyes twinkled at her husband. "Come here, Ricki." She took a last gulp of coffee, stuffed the newspaper into the briefcase resting against her high-heeled shoes, then gave Ricki a big hug. "Good luck today. This is exciting! The first day of junior high!"

The words made Vanessa's most recent bite of pancake stick in her throat. She felt better, though, after Ricki's mother gave her a giant hug, too, adding a reassuring pat on the arm. "Sweetie, it will be wonderful. You'll see!"

Vanessa tried to smile.

12

In half an hour, she and Ricki stood on the curb in front of a huge, brown brick building. Andy had just let them out of his van. An orange sign over the enormous double doors read, ROOSEVELT JUNIOR HIGH SCHOOL.

Dad leaned across the front seat, and he aimed one of his cheery grins at them. "Break a leg!"

"Huh?" Ricki scrunched up her nose.

Vanessa explained, "Show business people say that to one another for good luck."

Ricki shrugged. "Oh. Well, thanks, Andy! I guess someday I'll get the hang of being a rock musician's stepdaughter."

He blew them kisses. "You'll do great today, okay? Don't worry."

Then he drove away.

Vanessa watched her father's blue van get smaller and smaller until it reached the far end of the street and turned. And disappeared. She felt about seven years younger, like a kindergartner, with first-day panic.

"Wow, this is cool!" said Ricki.

Vanessa turned to find her pulling her big, fancy camera out of her backpack. "What are you doing?"

"I'm going to take pictures of all the kids going in through the doors. Those big, big doors and those little, little kids."

"They're not little," said Vanessa. "They all look older than us."

"I mean, little compared to those doors. See?" Ricki started snapping the camera. This was going to be great. New people, new things to photograph!

13

"We're going to be late," Vanessa warned.

Ricki kept snapping pictures all the way into the building. Vanessa kept her eyes on the sheet of paper in her hand, her class schedule. Reading it helped her feel less nervous about the crowds of unfamiliar kids all around her. But it made her more nervous about the day ahead. First period, homeroom, Ms. Darrow. No Ricki. Ricki had Mr. Echeverria. Second period, social studies. No Ricki. Ricki had science. And so on, until prealgebra class in the afternoon. Only one class together all day!

It was terrible. Vanessa felt alone. There would be no Ricki, just lots of new kids, new teachers, strangers all day long!

"Hi!" called a voice from somewhere in the crowd.

Vanessa looked up but didn't recognize a soul. There was a boy with a crew cut, a girl wearing peace beads, another boy with acne, and they were all taller and seemed much, much older than her.

"Hey, look who's here!" exclaimed Ricki, yanking on Vanessa's sleeve.

A dark-skinned, pretty, very familiar face appeared in the crowd.

"Louise Ann!" cried Vanessa.

"Hello, you two! How're you doing? Are your teeth chattering? Knees knocking?" Louise Ann did a demonstration of the symptoms. Then she broke into a laugh. "Mine are. I'm terrified." She fingered one of her cornrow braids.

"About junior high? Me, too!" Vanessa confessed.

Ricki, who had been busy snapping pictures of

14

Louise Ann's performance, now took a picture of Vanessa's frown.

"Are you going to carry that thing around all day?" Louise Ann asked.

"My camera? Sure. I signed up for the photography minicourse."

"Hmm." Louise Ann shook her head and grinned. "I can already tell this is going to be one interesting year!"

For the first time all morning, Vanessa giggled. Half her nervousness had vanished at the sight of Louise Ann. Standing with her and Ricki gave her the comfortable, homey feel of last year at Kennedy, where they and Dani de Avila and Kimberly Morris always ate lunch together and played at recess.

"Well, I gotta go now," Ricki was saying. "My homeroom is supposed to be upstairs somewhere. I'd better go find it."

Louise Ann nodded. "This place is so big! I already checked out my homeroom. It's in classroom number 112, down this hall."

"Really? That's mine, too!" Vanessa cried.

Louise Ann smiled, lighting up her chocolate brown eyes. "Fantastic! Let's go!"

Homeroom, Vanessa decided, was not too bad. Ms. Darrow, a dark-haired, soft-spoken teacher just a couple of inches taller than Vanessa, said she knew how strange everything must seem on the first day at a new school but promised it would get better, even before the end of the week. She went over a map of the school and read through the student handbook, chuckling with her students at rules like: No Chewing

Gum Under Desks and No Unnecessary Time In Restrooms.

Afterward, Vanessa felt odd walking out of homeroom and down the hall to another classroom for social studies. Different teachers, different classrooms. Vanessa wondered if she'd ever get used to the change from intermediate school.

By the time fourth period came along, though, she had started to get used to it—the switching and all the different teachers and the crowds of strangers in every class. And maybe, she thought, she wasn't the only shy, worried person around. All the seventh graders were new to the school. And the eighth graders were only one year older, not really as old as they'd seemed at first.

At lunchtime, Vanessa walked alone down the stairs and up the hall toward the cafeteria. Last year, she had always walked to lunch with Ricki. The second she reached the cafeteria she started feeling nervous again. The room was gigantic—an echoing cavern filled with hundreds and hundreds of total strangers. Where would she sit? What if she couldn't find anyone she knew?

Vanessa stood frozen at the doors, jostled by the crowds of people hurrying to lunch. Somebody shoved past her so hard she smacked her elbow on the door frame.

"Oh, 'scuse me!" the person said, then went on talking with some other kids.

The somebody had two long black braids.

"Ricki!" Vanessa called above the roar of voices.

The braids whirled around like a propeller. "Vee?

16

Hi! That you just standing there? Well, come on. Let's have lunch."

Before she knew it, Vanessa was swept into the stream of people pouring into the cafeteria.

"Meet Marsha," said Ricki, "and Amy and Hector, from my science class. This is Vanessa, my sister."

Leave it to Ricki, Vanessa thought, to make three new friends by lunch!

"Your sister?" Marsha asked. "You two look really different."

Ricki laughed. "Yeah, see, we were twins, but we got tired of looking exactly alike, so we wear these disguises. Right, Vee?"

Vanessa and the other girls giggled. Hector looked like he believed it.

"We're stepsisters," Vanessa explained to reassure him.

While they waited in the milk line, Ricki took pictures. When Hector and Amy and Marsha went to sit with friends from their intermediate school, Ricki took pictures of them. She even took a picture of the empty table where she and Vanessa finally sat down.

"Our first junior high lunch table!" she said.

Vanessa shook her head. "You act like it's the Academy Awards."

"Well, you took half an hour to decide what to wear this morning."

"I was nervous."

"You can say that again!" Ricki grinned. "It's only school, Vee. Hey, look! Here come Dani and Louise Ann."

17

Vanessa frowned. "Who's that girl with them?"

A blond girl with rosy pink skin and bright blue eyes walked beside Dani. She looked super-healthy and fit, thought Ricki, as if she had just finished jogging around the park. Then Ricki peered closer, because there was something kind of familiar about the girl.

"Wait," she said, craning her neck forward. "That's not—It is! It's—"

"*Kimberly?*" asked Vanessa, eyebrows raised.

"Hi, Vanessa and Ricki," the girl answered softly.

"Wow, Kim! You look so . . . so different! What happened?" asked Ricki.

"She doesn't just look different," added Louise Ann. "She looks great."

Kimberly giggled, hiding her braces behind her hand. "I do?"

Petite Dani's shiny cap of black hair bobbed as she nodded. "You do! Kimberly spent the summer with her father. He is a ranch hound in Wyoming," Dani explained in her Filipino accent.

"Not ranch *hound*," said Louise Ann. "Hand. Ranch *hand*."

"Oh, yes. Hand. Isn't that interesting?"

Dani and the others crowded around the table with their lunches.

"You really do look good, Kimberly," said Vanessa. "Did you get lots of fresh air and exercise?"

Kimberly nodded. "That's what my father says— that I needed some fresh air. Every night we had to get to sleep right after dark, about nine o'clock, so

18

that we could wake up before dawn. We had these huge breakfasts, then worked all morning, had huge lunches, and then huge dinners, too, after working all afternoon.''

"Sounds like you worked and ate and slept,'' said Ricki.

"But it was fun.'' Kimberly smiled. "And on weekends we went swimming at a lake and to some barn dances, and I learned to ride a horse and take care of her, and I saw a foal born.''

"A baby horse!'' said Louise Ann. "Wow. Compared to that, my summer was a total dud. All I did was help my mother and aunts at their African imports shop in San Francisco. That and my piano lessons.''

"I went home with my parents to the Philippines for a family reunion,'' reported Dani.

"Did you see your boyfriend there?'' Kimberly asked.

"Rafael?'' Dani shook her head. "He is history. We are only friends now. He was too lazy about answering my letters. I do not want a lazy boyfriend.''

"Well, what did *you* two do all summer after your parents got married?'' Louise Ann asked.

Ricki and Vanessa looked at each other.

"Our summer was complicated,'' answered Vanessa.

"It would take forever to tell it all,'' Ricki agreed.

"Well . . .'' Dani glanced at her watch. "We have thirty minutes.''

While they all gobbled their lunches, Ricki de-

19

scribed the wedding of her mother to Vanessa's father. Vanessa told about how it was interrupted by a telegram from her mother in Hawaii, and how she and Ricki worried that something would go wrong and change their parents' minds about getting married. But all Vanessa's mother said in the telegram was that she'd come to visit soon.

Then Ricki explained about Aunt Allegra and the weird nighttime noises they thought might be a ghost.

"In my closet we found love letters," said Vanessa, "that a guy named Emmett Tibbs wrote to Clementine Hewitt, a girl who lived in our house back in the 1930s!"

"You're kidding!" gasped Louise Ann.

"Later in the summer our next-door neighbor, Dr. Rosen, told us that Emmett drowned in a shipwreck or something," Ricki went on, "and Clementine's family thought he was haunting their house—which is our house now!—because they heard those noises, too. So they moved out."

"Then do you really have a ghost?" Kimberly's blue eyes widened.

Ricki grinned. "Yeah. Lots of them. They're gray and black and furry and have masks over their eyes."

Louise Ann smiled. "Oh, raccoons! We had some, too, once."

Vanessa continued the story. "And it turns out that Clementine Hewitt lives down the street now. Can you believe it?"

"What *I* can't believe is that anyone would write *her* love letters!" Ricki shook her head. "She's so rude."

20

"Not very friendly," Vanessa agreed. "She yelled at us when we went down to talk to her. But anyway, here's the most important news! I got a dog! His name is Kirby, and he's really adorable and smart, and he—"

A loud shout interrupted her. She and the other girls all dropped their forks and sandwiches and swiveled around toward the noise.

"I don't believe this!" whispered Louise Ann.

"For Pete's sake, not again," Ricki rolled her eyes.

"Oh, look, there's a whole group of them this year!" said Dani.

Their eyes focused on seven girls gathered around the drinking fountain.

"Go, go Cougars! Way to go!" chanted one of the girls, tall and red-haired.

All six of the rest chimed in with her, waving their arms and kicking their legs in unison. "Go-o-o-o Roosevelt Cougars!"

The whole group leaped high into the air and gave one more shout. "Cougars go-o-o-o to the top!"

"Look! There is Courtney Haines from our old school," Dani pointed out.

"She didn't waste any time making pals of the cheerleaders, did she?" noted Louise Ann.

"She really wants to be one of them," Kimberly whispered.

"Ho-ho! Hey-hey!" the tall redhead began chanting again. "Roosevelt Cougars are here to stay!"

Ricki wiped her mouth on a napkin and jumped up from the table.

"Where are you going?" asked Louise Ann.

Ricki grabbed her backpack and pulled her camera out. "It's a photo opportunity!"

"Oh." Vanessa chewed on the inside of her cheek. "Oh, no."

In three seconds flat, Ricki stood next to the cheerleaders, clicking away. She kneeled in front of them and angled the camera sideways. Next she climbed up on a nearby lunch table to snap shots from above.

The red-haired cheerleader stopped cheering. She planted her knuckles on her hips. She glared up at Ricki, then blew hard on a big football-shaped silver whistle tied around her neck. "Stop!"

All the girls behind her fell silent.

"What," she asked Ricki, "do you think you're doing?"

Watching from the lunch table, Vanessa froze. "Oh, no," she whispered again. The first day of junior high, already a disaster.

Everyone else froze, too. Except for Ricki.

Chapter 3

Ricki let out the breath she'd been holding and kept snapping pictures. At first it was kind of a surprise to hear someone yelling at her, but she didn't intend to let that get in her way.

"Hey! I said cut it out!" shouted the cheerleader.

"Who, me?" asked Ricki, snapping another shot of the redhead, whose blue eyes glared in her direction. She knew she should put her camera down, but she didn't really want to.

"Ricki Romero! You listen to Tiffany right now," shouted one of the girls, a blonde in a short skirt. "Tiffany Logan is the *head cheerleader* of this school."

"Oh, hi, Courtney. How're you?" Ricki grinned and waved. Then she clicked her camera again.

"Get rid of that camera, now!" ordered Tiffany.

Ricki moved the lens away from her eye. "Why?"

"Because we didn't authorize pictures," said Tiffany, "that's why."

"Authorize pictures?" Ricki repeated.

"Yes." Tiffany nodded. The crowd of girls behind

23

her nodded, too, as if it were part of a cheer. "We don't allow just *anyone* to take pictures of us."

"You're kidding," said Ricki.

"Who are you?" Tiffany demanded.

Ricki squinted at her. This was too much. She couldn't decide whether to laugh out loud or to throw a tomato. How stuck up could you get? "Name's Ricki Romero." She hopped down off the table and popped the lens cap onto her camera. "I'll stop. But it's a shame. You looked good. Real coordinated and everything. I got some great shots."

"You did?" asked one of them, a short girl with curly brown hair.

"Sure," said Ricki. "Yeah, I was going to give you copies of them, too. As, um, souvenirs. Yeah, souvenirs. You know, from the first day of school and all." Ricki smiled big.

"You were going to give them to us?" asked one of the other girls.

"Well, yeah," said Ricki. "Um, I was going to, but now . . ."

"Oh, please, Tiffany," said another one of the cheerleaders, "let her give us some pictures. We don't have any group photos yet this year."

Ricki tapped a finger on her chin. "Well, I would, except . . ."

"What?" asked Tiffany, frowning. "Except what?"

"Well, except I need to finish this roll of film before I can get it processed, and . . . I've still got about five shots left, so . . ."

"You can finish them now," said the curly haired girl. "Oh, can't she, Tiff?"

Six pairs of eyes glued on Tiffany, followed by a chorus of, "Yeah! She can take more pictures of us, can't she, Tiff? Just a few more?"

Tiffany sighed loudly. "Well, all right. Just a few more."

Ricki grinned. "Okay, everybody. Do another cheer."

The girls formed two lines, one behind the other.

Back at the lunch table, Louise Ann shook her head. "Would you look at that? They're *beaming* for that camera now!"

Vanessa giggled. "Look at Courtney. She keeps trying to move up to get in the picture."

"And the chief cheerleader, Tiffany," said Dani. "She is looking at the camera with a big smile like the woman on 'Wheel of Fortune.' "

Kimberly watched in wide-eyed fascination.

"That Ricki," said Louise Ann, shaking her head again.

Vanessa smiled, deeply relieved. Leave it to Ricki to turn disaster into success.

After school, Ricki climbed into the backseat of Andy's old van next to Vanessa, grinning ear to ear.

"Hey, this is great!" she said. "Feels like we've got a chauffeur. Other years I had to ride the bus."

Andy laughed. "Well, it's nice to know someone appreciates me. Vee always complained, because I wouldn't *let* her ride the bus."

"It seemed like more fun," said Vanessa.

25

"Speaking of fun, how did school go today?"
Andy asked. "Excitement? New friends?"

"Ricki made about a million new friends,"
Vanessa reported. It was hard to keep an edge out of
her voice. While waiting for her dad after school,
Ricki had talked to Marsha and Hector, and then to
a girl from her English class, then another from her
photography class. All day, it seemed, Ricki had
talked to nearly every kid in the school—except
Vanessa.

Ricki slapped her knee in a laugh. "Weren't those
cheerleaders a riot? Did you see them edging each
other out of the way for poses?"

"I couldn't believe how you stood up to that head
cheerleader after she yelled at you. I would have been
mortified."

Ricki rolled her eyes. "She's not a god, you know.
Anyway, how about *you,* standing up to old pickle-
face Clementine last week? I was mortified then."

"Speaking of Clementine," Andy interrupted, "I
called the animal shelter people again today to let
them know our raccoon family is still in the attic.
They're sending out officers this afternoon at four."

"Oh, gosh." Vanessa checked her watch. "It's
three-thirty. Can we hurry, Dad? I want to watch
them. How are they going to get the raccoons out of
that crawl space?"

"No idea." Andy shrugged. "They said they may
not even try to get them out, depending on the situation. It's apparently best for the animals just to leave
them alone. Anyway, they mentioned something
about taking them to Clementine Hewitt's afterward,

26

depending on what age the animals are and whether or not they can be released in the wild.''

The minute they got home, Vanessa ran upstairs to change, so that she'd be ready when the shelter officers got there. Ricki headed straight to the kitchen for a snack.

A woman with spiked-up green hair stood at the kitchen sink, mixing up a bucket full of sticky-looking orange goo.

"Hi, Zinna," said Ricki. Last summer she would have been too awed by Andy's artist and musician friends to say even that much to one of them. Most were kind of odd looking. But she was finally getting used to them. Especially since the first big family powwow when hours were decided upon for all Andy's wild friends.

"Oh, hello, Ricki," said Zinna. She smiled, showing the gold half-moon carved into one of her front teeth. Her black leather jacket had little metallic half-moons on it, too. "Did you just get home?"

Ricki nodded, taking the milk carton from the refrigerator and a box of peanut butter cookies from the cupboard. It used to bug her to have Andy's friends around. So what if their own apartments were too small to work in? Having them in *her* house was a pain. Over the summer, it really got on her nerves the morning when Gordon, Andy's music composing partner, dropped in unexpectedly while she was still in her pajamas. Another morning, she woke up to find the bathroom sink full of Zinna's orange collage goo. Then she stubbed her toe on Bernard's totem pole carvings in the den.

27

"Want a cookie?" Ricki asked Zinna.

Zinna wiped a smudge of goo off her freckled nose. "Okay, thanks."

The doorbell rang. Carrying one cookie in her mouth, one in her hand, and a tall glass of milk in the other, Ricki made it only halfway to the front door before she heard Vanessa and Kirby clambering downstairs.

Vanessa flew to the door in front of Ricki and peeked through the peephole. "It's them!"

Kirby wagged his tail. Then he caught sight of Ricki's cookie and wagged it even harder, licking his lips.

While Vanessa's back was turned, Ricki gave him half of it. He licked her palm in thanks.

"Yuck," she muttered.

Vanessa opened the door.

"Hi," she said to a man and a woman in green uniforms. "You're here about our raccoons?"

A tall woman with long, sand-colored hair smiled. "I'm Corporal Linda Graham, state humane officer. This is Officer Jack Lu." She gestured to her partner, a young man with friendly black eyes. "A Mr. Andrew Shepherd called us out."

"That's me." Andy stood behind the girls. "Thanks for coming. We've got raccoons in our attic."

Corporal Graham nodded. "Common, especially here in the more wooded areas."

"Girls, would you mind showing the officers where our little friends hang out?"

Silly question, thought Ricki. Vanessa was bursting at the seams.

Andy went back to work with Gordon in the living room. The officers, carrying long leather gloves and two cagelike wire crates, followed Vanessa and Kirby upstairs. Ricki was about to follow, too, when the phone rang.

"I'll get it," she yelled. "Tiff's supposed to call about the pictures."

. *Tiff?* Vanessa wondered in amazement. Only one day in junior high and Ricki was already getting calls from the head cheerleader, and calling her Tiff!

"Hey, I remember this guy," Officer Lu said, rubbing Kirby's ears. "Didn't he spend some time at the shelter over the summer?"

Vanessa nodded. "We found him down the street, but we had to give him up, because my stepmother thought she was allergic to dogs, but then she found out that she wasn't, so she went and got him back."

They reached the landing at the top of the stairs.

Corporal Graham smiled down at the dog. "Happy ending, huh? Well, sorry, big guy, but you can't come up to the attic with us, okay? You'll scarc the whiskers off those raccoons."

"Oh," said Vanessa. "I'll put him in my room. There's the stairwell to the attic, through that little door. I'll be right back, without Kirby."

"Good idea," agreed Corporal Graham.

A minute later they were all assembled in the attic next to a pile of plywood and a toolbox.

"Our parents want to remodel up here, but they don't want to disturb the raccoons." Vanessa pointed to a low, narrow opening in the south wall. "They're in that crawl space. We can hear them at night. It sounds really spooky sometimes, as if they're right in the hall between our bedrooms, because the sound carries through the vents."

"Yup. These guys can make an awful lot of noise," said Officer Lu.

To back him up, a loud chittering echoed out of the crawl space. Then came a high-pitched, gurgly scream.

Corporal Graham frowned. "Have you been hearing that sound very often? The distress call?"

"Is that what it is?" Vanessa asked. "My sister heard it last night, I think."

"Hmm." Corporal Graham pulled a long black flashlight from a holster on her hip. "We'd better trap the mother, then have a look at her kits."

"Sounds like one of them may be in trouble, huh?" asked Officer Lu.

Corporal Graham nodded.

Half an hour later, one of the wire crates, which the officers explained was a humane trap, contained a very frightened mother raccoon. Silver and pudgy, with a black bandit marking across her eyes, she was one of the most adorable creatures Vanessa had ever seen. But her eyes flashed, and her jaw gaped wide, hissing and snarling. The can of tuna she had ambled into the trap to eat now sat untouched, because the trap door had snapped shut right behind her, making her fur stand on end. Nor did she look very happy about Officer Graham poking into the crawl space where her family was with a flashlight.

"See anything?" asked Officer Lu. He mopped his forehead with an orange bandanna.

"Not yet. I'm going in a bit."

Vanessa and Officer Lu squatted at the entrance to the crawl space, waiting.

After a moment, they heard a muffled voice. "Oh, gosh."

"Whatcha got?" Officer Lu flicked on his own light and shone it into the passage.

"Looks like one of these little guys has been exploring," answered Corporal Graham. "Got itself stuck."

"Need a hand?" asked Officer Lu.

"I think—" Corporal Graham began.

Another round of the kits' loud chittering exploded down the passage, interrupting her. Vanessa saw the mother raccoon's back arch in worry about her babies.

"There. I've got him." Corporal Graham came crawling backward out of the passage and presented Officer Lu with a small, black, squirming form. "There's a gap in the floorboards in there, and guess who found it. He was hanging halfway into it, held up only by the width of his little shoulders."

"Poor guy," said Officer Lu. "Looks dazed. Think he's been stuck here a while?"

Corporal Graham nodded. "Probably a couple of days. He's going to need attention down at Clementine Hewitt's. And the rest of the family needs to be relocated before more of them decide to get adventurous."

After placing the raccoon kit in the second crate,

Officer Lu and Corporal Graham caught its three littermates with a long-handled net.

"There we go." Corporal Graham fastened the latch on the kits' cage. "You guys are all tucked in now."

"Don't worry," Vanessa clucked softly to the mother. "You'll be reunited with your children really soon. Won't she?"

Corporal Graham smiled. "We'll take them all down to Clem's and have her evaluate the kit. If it's okay, we'll take the whole family out to a state park and give the mom a chance to make a new home. She may have to do it without the one kit, though, if he needs extra care from Clementine."

"We'd better be on our way now," said Officer Lu, picking up the mother's cage.

Corporal Graham took the other one. "Thanks for your help, Vanessa."

"Oh, you're welcome," she answered. "Thanks for rescuing them." She showed the officers to the front door. As their truck rumbled away, she let out a long sigh. The baby raccoons had been so cute, she hated to see them go. As she gazed out over the front lawn, Vanessa noticed something orange lying on the front path. Officer Lu's bandanna. It must have fallen from his back pocket.

Oh, my. Vanessa chewed on her cheek. The responsible thing to do would be to go to Clementine's and return the scarf to Officer Lu. Yet the thought of seeing Clementine Hewitt again made her cringe. Her dad would probably say no, anyway.

Or so Vanessa thought. When she showed him the

bandanna, he actually suggested she run it down to Miss Hewitt's.

Well, at least she'd get to see the raccoons again, she told herself.

On her way through the hall, Vanessa saw that Ricki was still on the phone. It was just as well, she decided. Ricki would definitely not want to go to Clementine's again. Not that Vanessa was crazy about the idea herself. She would just give Officer Lu his bandanna, take another look at the raccoons, then leave.

Arriving at Clementine's, Vanessa was relieved to see the humane officer's truck still parked in the driveway. Corporal Graham and Officer Lu stood amidst the thick greenery on the patio, holding the cages. Clementine held a baby raccoon.

"This kit is severely dehydrated and in shock. He'll need a lot of attention. What do I want with another mouth to feed?" Clementine grumbled at Corporal Graham. At the same time, she held the raccoon kit close to her chest, running a finger softly from its tiny ears to its fuzzy nub of a tail. "And what do *you* want?" she demanded of Vanessa.

"Oh—" Vanessa stammered. "I—I wanted to return this to Officer Lu. You dropped it in our yard."

"Thanks." He grinned, taking the bandanna. "Nice of you to bring it."

"Are you overloaded, Miss Hewitt?" Corporal Graham was asking.

"Overloaded? Hah!" Clementine's yellow teeth glinted. "When am I *not* overloaded here?"

33

Officer Lu glanced at Vanessa and rolled his eyes. "Would you like us to take the raccoon kit to the shelter?" Corporal Graham offered.

Clementine's head shook in a severe "no." "You don't have the setup to care for it there, and you know it." She went on stroking the kit.

Corporal Graham sighed. Then, spotting Vanessa, she seemed to get an idea. "Listen, Miss Hewitt. If you're overworked here, and we obviously can't properly care for this raccoon at the shelter, how about getting a volunteer to help?"

"Help? That's a joke. You think I want some nitwit traipsing in and out of here?"

"I think you could find a capable assistant. Matter of fact, you have a possibility right here." Corporal Graham nodded toward Vanessa.

Clementine's eyes wheeled on her.

"Me?" Vanessa whispered, glancing desperately at Corporal Graham.

"I think it could work out well," insisted the officer. "You're interested in animals, right, Vanessa? And Miss Hewitt could use help, so—"

"I don't need help!" barked Clementine.

Her sudden outburst caused the kit she held to let out a little yelp. That led its brothers and sisters in the cage to start whimpering, too, and prompted their mother to croon out a miserable response. Their cries all grew louder and louder, so that Vanessa could hardly even hear herself think.

"They sound hungry," shouted Officer Lu above the racket.

"That's exactly what they are," Clementine

shouted back. "And you have kept them from being fed. This one needs fluids right away."

"Okay, then we'll be going now," said Corporal Graham. She picked up the crate holding the mother raccoon.

Officer Lu took the one with the kits, and they both set off up the driveway.

For a moment Vanessa lingered, amazed at how much noise a few small animals could make.

"Well," Clementine bellowed at her, "don't just stand there. Are you coming or not?" She turned and headed into the house.

Vanessa gave the question a very brief moment's thought, then followed Clementine inside.

Chapter 4

"Hey, Alison!" Ricki called to a brown-haired girl with glasses passing the lunch table. "How're you doing?"

The girl waved. "Hi, Ricki."

"She's an eighth-grader in my photography class," Ricki explained. Vanessa, Louise Ann, and Kimberly sat with her in the cafeteria Wednesday afternoon. "Oh, and there's Caroline from my soccer team. Hi, Caroline!"

Caroline waved back. "Hi, Ricki!"

Louise Ann took a bite of her sandwich and shook her head. "How come we've only been in this school a week and you already know everybody, Ricki?"

Ricki shrugged. "Not everybody."

To Vanessa, it seemed she did. Ever since they had walked into the cafeteria, Ricki hadn't stopped chatting with passersby, or the kids at the next table, or even people halfway across the room.

It was amazing.

"Ricki's really popular," said Kimberly quietly.

"You can say that again," Louise Ann agreed. "She even won over the cheerleaders."

"Some folks find it hard to resist a camera." Ricki grinned smugly. "Anyway, they make interesting photo subjects. All the jumps and stuff cheerleaders do. Stuck up or not, they sure are athletic."

"Courtney's going to try out," said Kimberly. "Everyone says she'll win one of the two seventh-grade spots."

Louise Ann nodded. "She's pretty good at it. She can do all the moves."

"Eeuu! What is *that*, Marco?" Ricki asked a boy holding a bowl of brown mush at a neighboring table.

"My latest invention," said Marco Jimenez.

"We're trying to see," explained Lester Washington, "how many different school lunch foods we can combine without causing an explosion."

Ricki watched Marco mix chocolate pudding and mashed potatoes.

Vanessa poked her in the ribs. "Look!"

"I know," said Ricki. "It's disgusting."

"No, not them," Vanessa whispered. "That!"

Ricki turned back to the table to see Kimberly's blue eyes growing round. Louise Ann's jaw had dropped. They all stared at two people walking hand in hand toward them.

"Holy kazoo!" Ricki whispered.

"Hello, everyone!" chirped Dani, pulling Randall Mott onto the bench next to her.

"Well, hello," said Ricki.

Randall, whose heavily freckled cheeks blushed to match his carrot red hair, mumbled, "Hi." He kept his eyes turned downward.

"You remember Randy, don't you?" asked Dani. "From our old school?"

The girls all nodded, still too shocked to speak.

After putting her lunch on the table, Dani stuck out her right arm. "Look what Randy gave me!"

A charm bracelet encircled her wrist, dangling two little silver hearts.

"Isn't it gorjayoose?" Dani giggled.

"Gorgeous," Louise Ann corrected her.

"Yes, gorgeous!" Dani giggled again.

Randall blushed ten times deeper.

This is so weird, thought Ricki. Randall had always acted about as tough as almost any of the boys. She had never imagined him blushing!

"Are you—" Kimberly stammered. "Are you and Randall—"

Dani slipped her arm through Randall's and snuggled up to him.

"We're going together," Randall announced. He lifted his eyes, but only for a second.

"*Going* together?" Ricki grinned. "Going where?"

Vanessa giggled, joined soon by Kimberly.

Louise Ann was the only one who stayed straight-faced. "I waited for you outside your math class this morning," she told Dani.

Dani nodded. "I walked with Randy. He waits for me after all my classes." She smiled up at him.

Randall broke into a grin, revealing the metallic sparkle of braces underneath.

"So you two are, like, boyfriend and girlfriend now?" Ricki asked.

"Today we decided," Dani explained. "Last week we became friends in science class, then Friday, Randy said, 'do you want to go together?' And today I told him yes." She smiled happily. "But I told him we must sit at my friends' table for lunch, always. He did not want to sit at a table only of girls. But my friends do not bite, do they?"

Louise Ann smiled, looking relieved.

Vanessa looked on, astonished. Only one week of junior high had passed, and already one of them had a boyfriend!

For a while no one talked. It took several minutes for the girls to adjust to the fact that there was a boy at their table. They ate their lunches in silence. Then Ricki again started calling out to friends passing by. Louise Ann mentioned that she had a piano recital coming up next month. Kimberly asked if anyone wanted to share her sour cream potato chips. Little by little, things went back to normal. Soon even Randall spoke a couple of sentences, telling Kimberly he would like some chips and asking Vanessa if she had started on the assignment for their English class yet. For the moment they all set aside the fact that Randall was the first boy ever to sit with them.

Ricki took a large bite out of her apple and was about to ask Lester and Marco how their experiment was coming along, when she noticed a funny, tickly feeling on the back of her neck between her braids. She scratched it. Then she felt it again, only this time it felt more annoying, as if something small and papery had just whizzed past her skin.

She turned around and didn't see him, although she knew he had to be there somewhere. Schuyler Simmons.

Still scratching the back of her neck, Ricki squinted at the sea of faces at the tables behind her. "All right, Schuyler, where are you? Stop peashooting."

Marco and Lester snickered and nudged each other. Then Ricki noticed a tuft of mouse brown hair sticking up above a corner of their table.

"There he is!" cried Kimberly in the same tone of voice she'd have used about a cobra or a vampire.

"Quit it, Schuyler," Ricki said calmly.

Schuyler stood up and shot another paper wad through his straw. It hit Ricki on the forehead and bounced off into Louise Ann's chocolate milk.

"Oh, gross!" groaned Louise Ann, sticking her tongue out.

Ricki glared at Schuyler. "How dense are you? I said, cut it out."

As she spoke she looked him over carefully. The guy was definitely the same Schuyler Simmons who had pestered her and the others so much last year at Kennedy. But maybe he had grown a little taller over the summer. And his hair actually looked clean, instead of greasy like last year.

One thing that hadn't changed, though, was the irritating, snide look on his skinny face.

Ricki considered the options on what to do if he shot at her again. Throw her apple core at him, grab his backpack and dump all the stuff out. . . . Anything she could think of would probably attract the attention of the two teachers who were supposed to be monitoring the cafeteria.

Schuyler didn't shoot at her again. Instead he shot Kimberly, who squealed, then Louise Ann, who yelled at him to stop. He was aiming for Vanessa when suddenly his hands dropped.

Ricki believed her glaring at him had worked. "You're a juve, Schuyler," she said, "a real juvenile." But then she realized he wasn't even looking at her. His eyes were glued on a spot just behind her.

Ricki turned. The spot was Tiffany Logan, surrounded by the other eighth-grade cheerleaders.

"Hello, Ricki," Tiffany said.

Out of the corner of her eye, Ricki noticed Schuyler stuff his straw into his back pocket.

"Hi, Tiff. How're you doing?" Ricki asked.

"Fine. I've come to say that our cheerleading squad approves of the photos you gave us, and we want you to take formal portraits of us at our first official practice next Thursday."

Ricki scrunched up her nose. "You do?"

"Yes. Our faculty sponsor approves, too. She says we can reimburse your film expenses out of our squad budget. The practice is next Thursday at three-thirty. See you there." Tiffany gave Ricki and the others a brief flash of her teeth, then turned to go.

"Wait," said Ricki.

Tiffany turned around.

"I didn't say I'd do it." Ricki studied a thumbnail.

Tiffany's blue eyes squinted. "Why wouldn't you?"

"Why should I?" Ricki gazed into the distance, as if considering the offer. Then she shrugged. "Oh, well. I guess I've got a little extra time next Thursday.''

It was kind of a goofy thing to do, Ricki admitted to herself later that afternoon. To photograph the cheerleading squad. Cheerleading was goofy. Tiffany was goofy, too. But the squad *was* going to pay for her film. And then her pictures might be published in the school yearbook.

All during soccer practice after school she day-dreamed about her future as a famous photographer. Big newspapers would hire her to cover space shuttle launches, and *National Geographic* magazine would send her on Antarctic expeditions.

When the soccer team car pool dropped her off at home, Ricki's daydream was interrupted by loud pounding noises coming from the attic. Andy at work again remodeling. The plan was to make the attic into a guest room.

"Hi! I'm home!" she called from the entry.

In a second she heard Andy clomping to the top of the attic stairs. "Hi! I'll be down in a minute."

Ricki headed for the kitchen. A couple of minutes later Andy arrived, shaggy brown hair coated with a layer of dust. "Well, good afternoon. How'd practice go?"

"Great. Coach says I can play forward this year." She sat at the table with a can of soda and a box of Fudgees cookies.

"Hey, that's terrific!" Andy washed his hands and joined her at the table.

Ricki popped a cookie in her mouth. She liked

42

having Andy around in the afternoons, coming home to him instead of to an empty house, as she used to before he and her Mom got married.

"Listen, Ricki, did you by any chance see Vee walking home on your way here?" Andy asked.

Ricki shook her head. "Nope. Is she at Clementine's again?"

Andy nodded. "For the fifth time in as many days. She went over there at three o'clock. I asked her to be back in an hour and a half. It's now four forty-five."

Ricki shrugged. "She's only fifteen minutes late. That animal stuff really gets her involved, you know. She's really into it. You can't pry her away."

"Well, we agreed on an hour and a half." Andy glanced at the big giraffe clock on the wall above the refrigerator. Two parallel lines of worry appeared on his nose between his brown eyes. Andy hardly ever frowned. Usually, he was the most cheerful person around.

It got on Ricki's nerves when he worried. After all, Vanessa hadn't gone to Siberia—just down the street. He and mom could be so protective! *Over*-protective. It was a pain.

"If she doesn't get here in the next fifteen minutes," Andy said, "I'll have to go down there."

Ricki rolled her eyes. "Oh, Clem would just *love* that. She is so friendly. She *loves* visitors." Before she could joke around more, Ricki noticed Andy frowning at her can of soda.

"Do you always drink that after school?"

43

Ricki shrugged. "I don't know. Well, no. I guess not. Not *every* day. Sometimes milk."

"That pop stuff is really bad for you." He pointed at the can as if it were radioactive. "Did you try those new cookies I got? Fruit juice sweetened. Fortified with sunflower and sesame seeds."

"I like *these* cookies," Ricki said.

Andy examined the Fudgees cookie label, reading the list of ingredients.

Ricki rolled her eyes again, preparing herself. Any second now Andy would start lecturing her about all the bad stuff she was putting into her system by eating Fudgees, just as he had about Choco-Chunks and SugarShot cereal and Cherry Sweetsticks.

The phone rang.

Ricki breathed in relief. Saved by the bell!

Andy snatched the wall phone off the hook. "Hello? Oh. Sure. Just a second." He handed the phone to Ricki. "For you. But please don't stay on long."

"For me?" Ricki took the receiver. "Hello?"

Andy picked up the newspaper and started reading.

"Hi, Ricki. This is Courtney Haines."

"Courtney Haines?" Ricki repeated.

"Why do you sound so surprised?" asked Courtney.

Ricki thought fast. This could be an important moment. She didn't want to let Courtney get the upper hand, as she had always tried to do back at Kennedy. At their old school, Courtney had always acted unbelievably stuck up. Maybe she was changing her ways. "Well, I was expecting someone else."

"Really? Who?"

"Oh, just someone," Ricki replied, trying to sound casual.

"A boy?" asked Courtney.

"Could be."

"Remember the day last year when you sat at my lunch table with me and Paige and Heather and Bill Mauser and Pearce Baldwin? Well, Bill and Pearce are at St. Theodore's Academy this year. Pearce calls me every day."

"That's nice," said Ricki, faking a yawn.

"I called you," Courtney went on, "because since you and I have been friends for so long, Tiff wanted me to give you a message."

"Oh?" Ricki decided not to point out that their friendship had consisted only of being at the same school for three years and sitting at the same lunch table once, when she had been having a fight with Vanessa.

"Tiff said to tell you the practice time has been changed to four o'clock."

"Oh. Fine." Ricki heard the front door open and close.

Andy jumped to his feet and headed for the hall. "Vee?"

"Hi, Dad!" called Vanessa cheerily.

"Well," said Courtney, "will you be there?"

Ricki kept one ear on her and the other on Vanessa and Andy. "Sure."

"Good. And . . . Ricki?" Courtney asked.

In the hall, Vanessa gazed up silently at her father, who was talking to her. Ricki couldn't hear him.

From the look on his face, though, she could tell it was serious talk.

"Yes, Courtney?" Ricki replied.

"You know I'm trying out for cheerleader, don't you? So I'd like these pictures to be good. It's important that I look good, okay? And that people see me in the pictures."

"Sure, Court. You'll look fine."

"I have to look good."

Vanessa's face was turning red. Ricki could see it all the way from the kitchen. Andy pointed his finger at his daughter.

"Right, Court. You'll look good, don't worry. Gotta go now, okay?"

"Well, okay."

Ricki hung the receiver back up on the wall. She stood very still, trying to hear Vanessa and Andy.

"I asked you to come back after an hour and a half, Vee, not two hours," he was saying.

"It was an hour and fifty-three minutes," Vanessa objected.

"Let's not split hairs, okay? The point is you had permission to go help out at Clementine's for a certain amount of time. Not all afternoon. And if you were going to be late, you should have called."

"Clementine doesn't have a phone." Vanessa's blond eyebrows pushed together anxiously.

"Then you should have come home."

Ricki felt awful for her sister. She hated to hear Vanessa get yelled at for nothing.

"There were new rabbits and a marsh hawk," Vanessa said. "Clementine needed help. I couldn't just leave. I didn't think a few minutes would make that much difference."

"Exactly. You didn't think," said Andy, stuffing his hands into his jeans pockets. "You didn't think about the fact that Anita and I worry about you girls."

Ricki decided that was her cue. She stepped into the hall.

"It's only a block down to Clem's," she offered.

"I know," answered Andy, glancing at her for only a second before turning back to Vanessa. "Otherwise we wouldn't let you two walk it. But you've got to stick to the time guidelines we give you, so that we can be sure of your safety."

Ricki shook her head. "We're twelve years old now, Andy, not little kids."

"That's true, but—" Andy began.

Ricki interrupted him. "We know all about crossing traffic and staying away from strangers."

"I know you do. Still, we all need to be responsible to each other and not cause unnecessary concern."

"Vanessa *was* being responsible," Ricki countered. "I mean, how much more responsible can you get than trying to save the lives of helpless little animals?" She glanced at Vanessa on her left, who still looked anxious.

On her right, Andy looked completely exasperated. He sighed. Then he rubbed a hand over his beard to his eyes to his dusty hair.

"You and I will talk more about this later," he said to Vanessa. "Right now I've got to get cleaned up for my five-thirty student.'' He sighed again, then opened his mouth as if to say something else. Instead, he just walked off, his footsteps a little heavier than usual.

Ricki looked at Vanessa and grinned.

Chapter 5

"Thanks for defending me this afternoon," Vanessa shouted above a pounding rock song beat. She and Kirby stood in the doorway to Ricki's room after dinner. To go in much farther would have meant a safari over the piles of clothes, books, and sports equipment strewn over the floor.

"No problem," Ricki replied from her dresser, out of which she had just pulled a stack of five T-shirts. "I know your dad was worried, but he didn't have to get *that* worried."

Vanessa watched as Ricki threw the T-shirts across the room to her bed. They landed like rag dolls.

At times like these, Vanessa was glad that she and Ricki no longer shared a room. All that mess, those ugly rock band posters and wisecrack bumper stickers on Ricki's walls, the loud music . . . It gave her a shiver.

"I know I shouldn't have let him worry," Vanessa went on, "but I honestly couldn't abandon Clem. You should see how busy she is."

"How about the letters? Has she said anything about them yet?"

Vanessa shrugged. "No. She's lived by herself for so long she doesn't talk a lot. Except to her patients. You ought to come down with me, Ricki. It's just amazing. So many animals."

"Wolves and bears and stuff?" asked Ricki.

Vanessa shook her head, finally making her way across the floor to an empty spot on Ricki's bed. Kirby curled up at her feet for a snooze. "There are no bears or wolves left anywhere around here. Mostly Clem gets birds. People find baby birds who have fallen out of the nest, or injured adult birds. Also we get squirrels, raccoons, opossums, rabbits, and right now we have a really cute little field mouse."

"A mouse? Yuck." Ricki scrunched up her nose. "Do you have to feed it with a bottle like you did the baby raccoon?"

"No, the mouse is an adult and seems to have been someone's pet. She's really tame and so adorable. We get other animals like that, too, even though it's against the law to keep wild species as pets. Sometimes people keep them anyway, then decide they don't want them anymore, so they set them loose. But the animals don't know how to take care of themselves in the wild and often get sick or injured. That's how they end up at Clem's. She's licensed by the state to treat them and get them ready to be released in the wild properly. It's called 'rehabilitation.' "

"Oh. And what's a species again? The kind of animal it is, right?"

Vanessa nodded. "Right. For instance, we're the human species. We're called Homo sapiens. And Kirby is *Canis familiaris,* a dog."

Ricki put a finger to her lips. "Hush. Don't tell him. It will come as too great a shock."

Vanessa laughed and scratched Kirby's head. Ricki threw a sixth T-shirt at the bed. The seventh, she pulled on over her tank top.

"What *are* you doing, Ricki?" Vanessa asked.

"Trying to decide what to wear to the cheerleader shoot tomorrow. How about this?" She held her arms out at her sides to model a yellow T-shirt that said DO I CARE? on the front in big red letters.

"Well, it's different." Vanessa leaned her head to the side.

Ricki pulled the shirt off. "I don't have anything to wear. Just T-shirts and jeans. That's not right for a professional photographer, is it?"

Vanessa's eyebrows rose in surprise. Ricki, of all people, worrying about what to wear? This was a switch!

"You're welcome to borrow something of mine, if you want," she offered. "If anything fits, that is."

"Hmm." Ricki tapped a finger on her chin. "That's an idea. But what could possibly fit? I'm four inches taller, about half a foot wider . . ."

"Come and look. Maybe we can find something."

Ricki dropped the DO I CARE? shirt on her bed and followed Vanessa and Kirby out. Then, the minute they entered Vanessa's room, she froze in her tracks. Rows of animals stared back at her from Vanessa's wall. The top row of posters was all puppies—cute brown puppies in baskets, cute white puppies peeking up over a wall, cute floppy-eared puppies playing tug-of-war with a blanket. Underneath them was a row of kittens, and then there were bunnies and ducklings. One poster, in the middle of it all, showed a mother Dalmatian dog with six adorably spotted pups. The caption read, "Your best friend's children have a fifty percent chance of survival. Fifty percent of all puppies and kittens born in the Bay Area never find a loving home. Get your pet fixed for life."

"Where did you get all this?" Ricki asked.

"Oh, I've had them for a while, but I just put them up yesterday," said Vanessa. "Clementine gets posters and things in the mail all the time."

"Clementine? You're kidding. Old Clem actually *gave* you something?"

"She's not as awful as she seems, once you get used to her. The reason she was so rude to us that day was because we had Kirby with us, and dogs scare wild animals. Anyway, she gets things in the mail from humane shelters and animal protection groups. How do you like them?" Smiling proudly, Vanessa gestured at the wall.

"Oh, um, nice," Ricki said, making herself smile back. The truth was that she'd rather jump in a lake than put up posters like that in *her* room. "Cute" was definitely not her thing.

She sat on Vanessa's neatly made bed. As usual the layers of ruffles and lace on the comforter felt like they'd swallow her up. Ruffles and lace weren't her thing, either.

"Let's see," said Vanessa from her closet. "You want something that looks professional, right? A skirt, maybe?"

"Not *that* professional. I don't know. Something . . ."

"How about this?" Vanessa pulled out a dark purple shirt, a birthday present from Ricki's Aunt Laura. "It's a bigshirt. You know, the oversized kind to wear over tights and things? On you it might be just right. You could button it all the way up and tuck it in like a business blouse."

"Hmm." Ricki got up. She held the shirt against her chest and looked in Vanessa's dresser mirror. "Yeah. Maybe tie a scarf at the collar, right?"

Vanessa smiled. "Sounds perfect. I've got a purple bandanna."

"Great! Thanks! Isn't this fun, Vee?" Ricki slipped the shirt on. "I mean, it's how we dreamed it would be. Being sisters, sharing stuff, being able to talk anytime we want."

Vanessa brought the bandanna. "We can even share parents when they're being unreasonable!" She smiled. It was wonderful to share and talk, to have rooms right next door to each other instead of across town. She remembered how she felt the week before, during the first days of school when Ricki found new friends and fit in so quickly at junior high. Vanessa had worried that she'd be left out. But things really hadn't changed, had they? She and Ricki were still sisters, after all.

"Hey, this fits great!" Ricki admired the shirt in the mirror, hands on hips. "I didn't used to like purple. But this isn't bad, is it?"

"It looks good with your dark coloring," Vanessa agreed.

53

Ricki was tying the bandanna around her neck when the phone rang.

"Here, set the knot to the side," said Vanessa, "like this."

"Ricki!" Andy's voice boomed up the stairs. "Call for you!"

"Okay! Hey, thanks, Vee. Gotta catch that call."

Vanessa watched as Ricki jogged downstairs. If this call was anything like the others, Vanessa knew, Ricki would be on forever. It could be Tiffany, Caroline, Alison, Marsha. . . .

Vanessa shut her closet door, smoothed the ruffles on her comforter, then sat at her desk to finish her science homework. At least, she thought with a sigh, there was no chance of any telephone calls interrupting *her*.

"Tiff, move over a step to the left. Good. Now, Bridgit, you get in front of Jeanne. There. Okay. Ready, everybody? Say 'fleas'!"

Ricki clicked the camera. It was her eighteenth photo of the cheerleaders that hour, and they hadn't even started their practice yet. The squad had insisted they wanted formal, posed pictures taken before they got sweaty and mussed in a workout.

"Hey, um, you—What's your name? Nicole? Lift your chin. Good. Hey, Courtney, move over. I can't see Bridgit. No, the *other* way. That's it." Ricki knew she sounded bossy but didn't care. It was the only way to get the shots she needed. The squad members and seventh-grade tryouts kept stopping in the middle of things to fix their hair or put on fresh

54

lipstick. And a couple of them, especially Courtney, kept trying to nudge their way into better spots. They were all being a pain.

Another pain was Kimberly, who stood like a star-struck zombie next to Ricki, watching the cheerleaders as if they were gods. Ricki had made the mistake of asking Kimberly to hold her equipment bag while she set up the tripod camera stand. Now Kimberly wouldn't budge. She was mesmerized.

Out of the corner of her eye, Ricki noticed Vanessa up in the bleachers, reading a book. At least she could try to be a little more sociable. For instance, why couldn't Vanessa try talking with Courtney's friends Paige and Heather, who sat just a couple of bleacher rows away? Instead, she acted as if having to stay after school with Ricki for the cheerleading practice was torture.

"Okay," Ricki said after snapping the last group shot. "I think I've got it all now. Did I miss anybody in the single shots?"

At that moment Kimberly stepped forward to hand Ricki the camera bag.

"Have *you* signed up yet?" asked Tiffany.

Ricki looked up. Was Tiffany talking to Kimberly?

Kimberly shook her head, blushing heavily. Tiffany kept staring at her.

"Well," Tiffany said, "you can sign the log later. Hurry up. Get your picture taken."

"But I—I was just—" Kimberly stammered.

Ricki shook her head to clear it. Did Tiffany actually think Kimberly wanted to try out? Never in a million years!

Ricki was about to try and straighten out the misunderstanding when another eighth-grade cheerleader, Bridgit, asked Kimberly, "What's your name?"

The answer came as barely a whisper. "K-K-Kimberly Morris."

"She's got that fresh, girl-next-door look, doesn't she, Tiff?" asked Bridgit.

Kimberly looked ready to melt in embarrassment.

Tiffany marched forward. She and Bridgit inspected Kimberly like ranchers at a cattle auction. Kimberly was the cow on the block. They crossed their arms, squinted at her, examined her up and down.

Tiffany finally announced, "She does. We've been looking for a blonde for the squad. Come here, Kimberly." Tiffany grabbed her by the arm and dragged her over to face Ricki's camera.

Bridgit removed Kimberly's ponytail holder and fluffed her hair to make it look a lot like all the other cheerleaders'.

"Okay, Ricki. Shoot," commanded Tiffany.

Blushing and blinking, Kimberly stared into the camera.

Ricki decided her friend resembled a rabbit in the paws of two foxes. "Do you want me to take your picture, Kimberly?"

"Well, of *course* she does," Tiffany snorted.

"Do you?" Ricki asked again.

Kimberly shrugged helplessly.

Ricki shrugged back and sighed. "Okay. Last chance. Here goes. Ready?"

Kimberly nodded, and Ricki snapped the camera.

Right afterward, a swarm of cheerleaders and tryouts surrounded Kimberly.

"Looked great," one of them cooed.

"Come over here, and we'll work on the cheers with you," Nicole said.

They folded her into their circle like a long-lost sister. It didn't seem to make a bit of difference that two minutes before, Kimberly had absolutely no intention of trying out. Two minutes before, she had been a shy nobody. Now she was a cheerleader tryout.

On Kimberly's face played a half-dazed smile. The group led her off to practice. Ricki shot another picture.

"Hot jeans, Kimberly," she heard one of the cheerleaders saying.

Ricki looked down at her own jeans and the purple "business" shirt Vanessa had lent her.

Not hot. Definitely not hot.

After shooting two more rolls of film of the practice session, Ricki slung the camera over her shoulder and headed for the bleachers.

Vanessa looked up from reading social studies. Finally, Ricki was finished! Any minute now her dad would come to pick them up. Slipping her book into her backpack, she climbed down the bleachers to join Ricki. But then Ricki disappeared, surrounded by a crowd of cheerleaders and tryouts.

"When will the pictures be ready?" Bridgit was asking.

"Can I get copies for my boyfriend?" asked Jeanne.

Vanessa finally spotted Ricki in the middle of it all, stuffing her camera gear into the bag, looking as cool and casual as ever.

"I'll have them all ready next week," she said. "Don't worry, you can get plenty of copies."

In the middle of the group, talking and laughing along, Ricki looked like she belonged.

Standing outside the circle, on the bottom step of the bleachers, Vanessa felt that as far as Ricki was concerned, *she* didn't even exist.

Chapter 6

Ricki slouched as low in her chair as possible. Maybe if she slouched low enough, Mrs. Minsk wouldn't be able to see her. And maybe if Mrs. Minsk couldn't see her, she wouldn't ask Ricki questions about the math homework. And maybe if Mrs. Minsk didn't ask her any questions about the homework, no one would know that Ricki didn't understand a bit of it.

"Ricki, would you come to the board and work problem three, please?"

Somewhere, Ricki had heard about heat-seeking missiles used in wars. They went straight for aircraft, because they had special radar equipment that sensed engine temperatures. Mrs. Minsk seemed to have that kind of radar, too, except hers sensed whether or not a kid had studied, or was paying attention, or understood something.

As Ricki approached the blackboard, Mrs. Minsk fired another missile. "And please explain it as you go along, will you?"

Queasiness jiggled Ricki's stomach. Her hands got

59

so sweaty that the chalk stuck to her fingers. Behind
her, she knew, twenty-seven pairs of eyes watched.

From her textbook, Ricki copied the problem onto
the board in small, faint handwriting.

*You are in a car 160 miles from Los Angeles. You
must be there in three hours. If you drive the first
hour at 50 miles per hour, how fast must you drive
the remaining two to get to Los Angeles on time?*

Ricki bit her lip.

"Now," said the teacher. "To begin with, what
are you looking for in this rate, time, and distance
problem?"

"Um, the speed you have to go for the last two
hours," Ricki answered in relief. At least Mrs. Minsk
was going to give her some hints.

"Good. So what do you do first?" asked Mrs.
Minsk.

Another attack of queasies hit Ricki's stomach. She
had absolutely no idea what to do first. Multiply
something? Subtract something? It was so confusing.
Last night she'd tried doing the homework problems.
Well, a few of them, anyway. But none made much
sense. Word problems always stumped her.

"I don't know," she finally admitted, keeping her
eyes on the board. If just one person snickered, she
vowed silently, she'd memorize the voice and get
them for it later.

One person snickered. That snicker Ricki knew
very well. Just you wait, Schuyler, Ricki promised
silently.

"Okay, let's step through the problem," said the teacher. "What information do we have?"

"I'm one hundred and sixty miles from Los Angeles," said Ricki. "I've got to get there in three hours."

"Right," said Mrs. Minsk. "What else?"

"Um, I go fifty miles an hour for one hour."

Mrs. Minsk nodded. "So your total distance is going to be one hundred and sixty miles, and you've already got fifty miles out of the way, right? How would you show that in an equation?"

Ricki bit her lip again. This was the part she hated. Showing things in equations.

"Think of it this way," suggested Mrs. Minsk. "How would you figure out how many miles you have left to go?"

Slowly, Ricki lifted the stick of chalk to the board and wrote:

$$160 - 50 = 110$$

"Yes." Mrs. Minsk nodded. "You've got one hundred and ten miles to go. And two hours left to drive them in, so what must be your miles per hour rate?"

Ricki wrote:

$$110 \div 2 = 55$$

"Exactly." The teacher smiled. "You must travel fifty-five miles an hour for the last two hours. Now, to show the whole problem in an equation . . ." She moved to the board beside Ricki. "What we want is one hour times fifty minutes plus two hours times x minutes, with x being the unknown. . . ."

A string of numbers and symbols appeared under Mrs. Minsk's chalk.

$$1(50) + 2(x) = 160$$

Within seconds, Mrs. Minsk had scribbled a whole column of other equations underneath it.

$$2x = 160 - 50$$

$$x = \frac{160 - 50}{2}$$

$$x = \frac{110}{2} = 55$$

The numbers and letters swam before Ricki's eyes. Mrs. Minsk kept stopping to make sure everyone understood. Everyone did, it seemed, except for Ricki. She could understand why she'd have to drive fifty-five miles on the way to Los Angeles, but she had no idea of what all those equations had to do with it. All she cared about at that moment was finishing that problem and getting back to her seat.

After the torture session at the board was over, Mrs. Minsk called on other students to work problems. Number eight went to Vanessa.

Ricki felt sorry for her. She knew how shy Vanessa could be, how she hated being the center of attention.

But Vanessa walked to the blackboard and worked the problem with quick, bold strokes of the chalk. She didn't look the least bit uneasy. Her voice sounded loud and clear as she explained, "If I were walking to the grocery store a mile away, I would have to walk at a rate of x miles per minute to get there before it closed in eight minutes."

When she ended up with the correct answer, one-eighth mile, Mrs. Minsk nodded in approval. Vanessa smiled and returned to her seat.

It was obvious that Vanessa understood every single thing about rate, time, and distance.

After class, Ricki walked out behind Vanessa and Louise Ann.

"What a great coincidence," Louise Ann was telling Vanessa. "Our teachers having a recital together."

"Which teachers?" asked Ricki, catching up to them.

"Oh," said Vanessa, "Louise Ann's piano teacher and my cello teacher are staging their students' annual recital together so we can get a nicer hall and accompany one another, too."

Ricki zipped up her backpack and slung it over her shoulder. "So you two are going to be in a recital together?"

Louise Ann smiled at Vanessa. "I might be assigned to accompany you."

The two of them went on chattering about the recital and which pieces they might be assigned to play and then about the Youth Orchestra auditions coming up in the spring.

Soon, Ricki had to turn upstairs to go to her social studies class. "Well, bye," she said. "See you at lunch."

Louise Ann and Vanessa waved, then went right on talking.

To Ricki, it seemed they barely even noticed that she had gone.

Vanessa walked past Dr. Rosen's front yard on her way home from Clementine's Monday afternoon, watching him inspect his lawn.

"Hi, Dr. Rosen," she called.

Slowly, he looked up and waved. After a puff or two on his pipe, he looked down at the lawn again.

Never had Vanessa seen anyone look so bored—or lonely. Every afternoon Dr. Rosen stood out in his front yard, as if hoping to catch a glimpse of a neighbor or a UFO or anything else interesting.

Unfortunately, Mariposa Lane wasn't very interesting at all. The neighbors mostly kept to themselves, and nothing exciting ever seemed to happen in their old, gloomy-looking houses.

Strolling up the front path to her own house, Vanessa admired the pretty new beds of red geraniums that her dad and Anita had planted. The welcoming white front porch led to the bright yellow house itself. One thing the place could not be accused of being was gloomy, Vanessa decided.

But as she opened the front door she began to change her mind. From inside came voices—not very

64

happy voices. In the kitchen she found Ricki and Anita, who wore a face as long as a telephone pole.

"I did not give you permission for this, Ricki. You know that very well," Anita was saying.

"But Mom, I didn't know I needed permission."

A loud sigh from Anita. "How could you *possibly* imagine that you wouldn't need permission to wear makeup? That's a pretty basic issue."

Makeup? Ricki wearing makeup? Vanessa wondered.

Anita stood near the sink, and Ricki sat at the table, back turned to Vanessa.

"I don't know," said Ricki, shrugging. "It didn't seem like such a big deal."

"Not a big deal? Ricki, you're only *twelve years old.*" Anita's voice, normally low and smooth, rose upward into the high and squeaky range.

"So?" Ricki replied. "Lots of seventh-grade girls wear makeup."

"I don't care what other girls do."

"See, a bunch of us were in the locker room before our after-school sports," Ricki explained. "And everybody but me was putting on makeup and fixing her hair. Bridgit, the assistant head cheerleader, asked if I wanted to borrow some lip stuff, and then Marsha said I'd look good in her shade of blush, and then everybody else pitched in, and I think I look great!"

"You don't," said Anita firmly.

Ricki shrugged again. "Well, *I* think I do."

"You are not to wear makeup yet, Ricki."

Another shrug.

"I'm serious," Anita insisted, voice growing even

higher. "For special occasions, maybe. But absolutely not for school."

"Why not?"

"You're just not old enough, honey. It's absurd for girls to start preening so early."

Still watching from the hall, Vanessa raised an eyebrow. This argument between Ricki and her mother sounded awfully similar to one Vanessa had had with her father—the one about working at Clem's. No one seemed to have noticed the girls were no longer children.

Vanessa took a step forward into the kitchen and cleared her throat. "Um, excuse me."

Still frowning, Anita looked at her. Then Ricki turned around.

Vanessa's mouth stopped working. All she could do was stare at the person who looked vaguely like her best friend and stepsister. Ricki had fluorescent orange lips, blueberry eyelids, and bubble-gum pink cheeks. Vanessa managed to catch her breath and go on. "Um, as I was saying, when *will* we be old enough?"

Anita sighed again. "We'll see when the time comes."

"But I was just wondering," Vanessa went on, "because, well, is there some magic age when we'll suddenly be mature? What will make us so different between now and next year or the year after that?"

"Vanessa, hon, I really don't think—"

"Yeah," Ricki put in. "How come I'll suddenly be mature enough to wear makeup later?"

Her mother's dark eyebrows lowered in another frown.

"What I mean is," Vanessa continued, "it's kind of hard on us right now to be treated like kids, because we're really not kids anymore, but no one wants to give us rights as adults."

"Vanessa, no one is depriving you or Ricki of your rights," Anita countered.

"That's how it seems," Vanessa said. "For instance, Ricki would like to wear makeup but is being told she can't, so . . . that is depriving her of her rights."

Anita shook her head. "Mothers do that, you know. We *do* have to make certain decisions. And we—"

The phone rang. Anita let out the deepest sigh yet and picked it up.

"Hello? Yes. All right. Just a moment." She covered the mouthpiece with her hand. "It's for you, Ricki. Actually, this is another problem we need to discuss. Ninety percent of our calls these days are for you. You're spending too much time on the phone."

"Maybe if we got call waiting service on the phone, it wouldn't be such a problem," Ricki suggested cheerfully.

Anita narrowed her eyes at her daughter. "As I said, you and I need to talk." She handed Ricki the phone.

With a bottle of apple juice from the refrigerator, Vanessa sat down at the table. After a moment her father walked in.

"Hi, everybody!" he said, smiling. He gave Anita

a kiss, another to Vanessa, then tapped Ricki's shoulder, whispering, "I'm expecting a call. You won't stay on long, will you?"

Ricki held up one finger to say she'd only be a minute. Andy made the "okay" sign back at her. But suddenly his jaw dropped open. He stared at Ricki, then looked at Anita. She nodded and let out a long sigh.

Sipping her juice, Vanessa decided to interrupt her father's moment of shock. "Dad, why don't we get call waiting?"

Her father didn't waste a second before shaking his head. "A lot of new technology these days makes our world even more rude and impersonal than it already was. Call waiting falls into that category. You're in the middle of a conversation, and another call comes in to interrupt you."

"It has the advantage, though," said Anita, "of preventing missed calls. People can always get through."

"Right," Andy agreed, "but it's just not worth the hassle of being interrupted."

Anita collapsed into a chair next to Vanessa. She slipped off her high-heeled shoes and started massaging her feet. "I wish you'd reconsider, Andy."

"I *have* reconsidered. I reconsidered the last time you suggested call waiting, and the time before that, and the time before that, and—"

"It's just so sensible," said Anita. "That's why I keep bringing it up."

Andy didn't respond. He poured himself a glass of juice.

"Bye, Alison," said Ricki into the phone. She hung up and was about to head for the table for some apple juice when she heard her mother's tense voice.

"I hate it when you do that, Andy."

"Do what?" he asked between gulps of juice.

"When you clam up. When you try to end a discussion just by being quiet."

"What am I supposed to say, Annie? I've already said I prefer not to have call waiting."

"Well, what if *I* want it?" Anita asked.

Ricki glanced at Vanessa, who was nibbling on the inside of her cheek, staring up worriedly at their parents.

Last summer the two of them would have done something about this. Ricki thought about all the times she or Vanessa had stepped in to stop their parents' arguments. They interrupted them, changed the subject, invented emergencies, did just about anything to get them to stop.

But not anymore. They had promised. Together, the girls had crossed their hearts in vows that they'd never butt in on their parents' arguments again. It just didn't pay.

Ricki wiggled her fingers to get Vanessa's attention. Vanessa nodded. She got up from the table. They both headed for the door, Kirby trotting at their heels.

"If it's that important to you," Andy was saying, "go ahead. Get call waiting."

"Then you'll be upset," Anita objected.

The girls heard no more as they hurried upstairs.

Vanessa whispered, "Look at Kirby."

69

The dog's head and ears drooped low. He blinked up at the girls with questioning eyes.

"He hates arguments," Vanessa translated.

"So do I. He looks about the way we feel, doesn't he?"

Vanessa nodded. "It's not at all as bad as it used to be, though. I mean, Dad and Anita hardly ever argue anymore. Neither do we."

"True," agreed Ricki. "We've all improved. Except, you and I fight more with our parents these days, don't we?"

"I guess there have to be *some* arguments," Vanessa said.

"Oh, by the way, thanks for sticking up for me in there. About the makeup, I mean."

Vanessa shrugged. "It's all right. Just out of curiosity, though, are you going to—"

"Wear it again?" Ricki shook her head. "No time soon. Mom's not going to go for it."

"I think you're right."

"How do you like it, anyway?" Ricki flashed a big smile, which highlighted her orange lips.

"The makeup?" Vanessa raised an eyebrow. "Well, it's um, fashionable."

"Just what I like in a sister," Ricki patted Vanessa on the back. "Honesty."

Chapter 7

Squirrels must be the messiest creatures on earth, Vanessa decided on a sunny Saturday afternoon. With a small brush she swept walnut shells, carrot chunks, and bits of apple out of a cage. Her back was getting sore, because she had to stoop to reach in. The cage's inhabitant, an eight-week-old squirrel with bright brown eyes and a bottle-brush gray tail, kept trying to hitch a ride on her wrist.

"No, no." Vanessa shooed him away. "Clementine says you have to stop being so tame."

"Don't talk to him," rasped a voice from behind her.

Vanessa was so startled that she bumped her head on the top of the cage door.

"He'll never be ready for the wild if you keep talking to him," Clem warned. "He'll go to every human he sees, and you know where *that* leads!"

Out of the corner of her eye, Vanessa watched Clem move about the huge backyard enclosure. It was fenced on all sides, covered by a green plastic roof, and crowded with small cages, large pens, and assorted crates and boxes full of animals.

After she finished the young squirrel's cage, Vanessa took his pile of trash to show Clem. "What are these little brown pellets?' she asked. "I didn't know we fed the squirrels cat chow."

Clementine's lips parted in a grin. "We don't feed the squirrels cat chow. That's poop. You should know that by now. Every animal in here poops."

Wordlessly, Vanessa stared at the pile in her hand. Poop. She was holding squirrel poop.

"It won't kill you," Clem said. "But use gloves if you want." She jerked a thumb to the right. "Over there, by the washbasin."

Vanessa looked at the gloves. They had holes in every finger. Sighing, she tossed the squirrel mess in a waste bin, then followed Clem to the pigeon pens.

That week there was a lot of cleaning to do. Clem had gotten behind on it, Vanessa knew, because of the new animals who had just come in. A cranky old opossum with an infected paw, a half-starved dove, a burrowing owl hit by a truck. All day while Vanessa was at school, Clem fed and treated them. Cleaning had to come last, even though Clem was extremely picky about cleanliness in the cages and pens. Her own house and yard may be a mess, but the animals were to be kept in style.

"I don't understand," said Vanessa as she and the older woman knelt beside a pigeon pen to change the newspapers, "how you've always done this alone. There's so much!"

Clem tucked an edge of the papers under a water bowl. "I've managed."

Vanessa decided not to say more. It might sound

72

like patting herself on the back, as if she were trying to point out what a great helper she was.

"It used to be different," Clem grumbled.

Vanessa wasn't sure she'd heard right or even that Clem had been talking to her. The old woman often muttered to herself.

"What do you mean?" asked Vanessa, shutting the door to the pen.

Clem grunted and creaked to her feet. "When I started doing this ten years ago, I'd get half a dozen, maybe a dozen animals a month. Now I get three times that many. People are building all over the county now, taking over the hills and woods, pushing animals out of homes they've had for centuries." With the back of her wrinkled hand, she shoved a lock of white hair away from her face. "Wilderness areas are getting smaller and smaller, fewer and fewer, so more and more displaced creatures end up here. And at the same time, I'm getting fewer and fewer donations."

"Donations?" Vanessa repeated.

Clem frowned. "I can't afford all the supplies for these animals myself, you know. I need money for it. Used to be I'd get some funding from the county, but that's dried up, thanks to all their budget cuts. This place . . ." Clementine waved her arm in a wide arc. "It isn't going to last forever."

"You mean, you might have to close down?"

"I mean I'll be taking in fewer animals, that's for sure."

"So what will happen to the animals you can't take in?"

Clementine shrugged. "You ought to know the answer to that. You're not a stupid child."

"The animal shelter will put them to sleep?"

"There may not be a choice for some of them."

Vanessa felt sick. She looked around at all the animals. One of the big, flapping mallard ducks in the small pond at the enclosure's far end let out a contented flurry of quacks. Two weeks ago he had been a skinny, hungry fledgling with a broken wing. She couldn't stand the thought of other animals like him not having a second chance.

"Well, don't just stand there, girl," barked Clementine, "let's get on with the cleanup."

Vanessa took a pile of soiled newspapers to the waste bin, then came back to Clem and asked, "Maybe if you asked for more money?"

"There was a time when I wrote letters, showed up at government board meetings, did all that sort of thing. I'm not going to beg anymore. Too old."

"What if you had more volunteers?" Vanessa pressed. "Not just me but others, too, and we all pitched in and—"

Clem shook her head so hard that her flabby cheeks jiggled. "It's enough I let you in. Hmph. Although I suppose *that's* worked out all right."

Vanessa saw the trace of a smile on Clem's face and realized that was probably the closest to a compliment the woman ever gave. It made Vanessa happy. But she couldn't stop thinking about how awful it would be if the wildlife rehab center had to close.

"There must be something we can do," she mumbled.

74

" 'We' is too many people," Clem snapped. "I'm doing all I can right now."

Vanessa had to admit she had a point. Clem really was very busy, spending all her days, sunup to sundown, and often much of her nights, too, caring for the animals. Vanessa had never met anyone so dedicated.

There just had to be a way to keep it all going.

Ricki loved the sound of crickets. Their chirping filled the warm October evening, letting her pretend it was still summer.

Out on the backyard deck Saturday afternoon, Ricki decided she couldn't be happier. There was just enough sunset light in the sky to have a cookout by. The smell of juicy barbecued hamburger on her plate mixed with the spices of mustard and pickles and all the fixings. She was starving!

"Mmm. This is delicious!" she mumbled in the middle of her first bite.

"Like it?" Andy grinned from across the picnic table. "Your mom made 'em. I just flipped 'em."

"It's your grandma's recipe," Anita said, "made with parsley and garlic. You've had them before, at Grandma and Grandpa's farm. So have you, Vanessa, one July Fourth when you went down to visit with us, remember?"

Vanessa nodded.

"You don't seem exactly ravenous tonight," Andy observed. "Feeling okay?"

Vanessa shrugged.

Her hamburger had not been touched, Ricki

75

noticed. Vanessa just nibbled on potato chips and lettuce.

"The hamburger's really great!" Ricki offered enthusiastically. "Try it!"

Vanessa shook her head. "I can't."

Puzzled, Ricki frowned.

"You can't?" Vanessa's father repeated.

Vanessa shook her head again.

Across the table, Anita leaned forward. "Why can't you, hon?"

Ricki watched her sister take a deep breath, then look at her hamburger. Silently, Vanessa pulled a pamphlet out of her sweater pocket. She held it up.

"Yuck!" cried Ricki. "What is that?"

"A veal calf," said Vanessa quietly. "It's a veal calf that has to live its miserable short life in a cage three feet long by two feet wide so it'll grow fat fast. It can't turn around or even groom itself. It develops sores and infections and—"

"Oh, gross!" Ricki interrupted, scrunching up her nose.

"Vee, hamburger is not made of veal," said her father.

"That's right, honey," Anita added. "Hamburger is beef."

"I know," Vanessa agreed in that same quiet voice. "Beef is the calf's mother."

Andy set his hamburger down, peering closely at his daughter. "Are you telling me you won't eat meat?"

"The thought of it makes me ill," Vanessa answered.

76

Ricki rolled her eyes. Cute little calf or not, how could anyone feel sick about eating something so delicious? She took another bite of her burger.

Anita frowned worriedly at Vanessa.

Resting his chin on a palm, Andy asked, "Vee, did you get that pamphlet at Clementine Hewitt's?"

"Yes. Clem got it in the mail from an animal rights group today."

"I see." Andy stroked his mustache with a thumb. "I think you've been spending a little too much time down there."

"At Clementine's?" Vanessa's eyebrows went up.

Andy nodded. "You've been there most of every afternoon for the past month. You've barely had time left over for your cello and homework."

"That's not true," objected Vanessa. "I get my work done and practice."

"Well, I think you need to cut down some on your hours at Clementine's," Andy said.

"That would be terrible!" Vanessa cried. "Clem really needs help now. There are more and more animals and less and less money—"

"Vanessa, none of that is your fault," said Anita. "You can only do your part to help."

"That's right," Andy agreed. "And your part at Clementine's needs to be a little smaller right now."

In the middle of another bite, Ricki glanced at Vanessa, whose chin thrust out stubbornly. At the same time, though, Vanessa's lower lip trembled, and her eyes looked moist with tears.

If there was one thing Ricki could not stand, it was seeing her best friend and sister cry. Quickly, she swallowed the mouthful of burger. "Why shouldn't Vee be able to help if she wants to?"

"We didn't say she couldn't," Andy answered. "She just needs to help a little less."

"How come?" Ricki pressed. "She's making great grades. And she practices her cello all the time."

"Ricki," her mother warned.

Andy interrupted. "Anita and I just feel Vanessa is spending too much time at Clementine's, which may not be the best of environments."

Vanessa looked up. "Best of environments? What do you mean?"

"Well," Andy said, "you've got to admit, Clementine is a little odd."

"You've never met her!" Vanessa protested.

"That's right," added Ricki. "You've just heard about her from us and Dr. Rosen. And even he said she's just kind of crotchety. I mean, lots of people seem weird at first. Some of your artist pals, for example, Andy. At first glance—"

"Ricki!" her mother cut in.

Andy smiled. "It's okay. Ricki's got a point there. People who seem weird aren't always weird. But still—"

"Vanessa's trying to save the lives," Ricki went on, "of sweet, innocent little animals. It's just not fair to—"

"Ricki, stop, right now." Anita's voice was quiet but firm.

Ricki knew that tone of voice. She shut up, quick.

"There's something I need to say." Anita folded her hands on the table.

78

"And I think I know what it is." Andy nodded. "We need a powwow."

"A powwow?" asked Vanessa. "But there's not one scheduled until—"

"We need to have it early," said Anita. "Things are getting out of hand."

"My thoughts exactly," Andy said.

"What do you mean?" asked Ricki.

"Which things are getting out of hand?" Vanessa chimed in.

"How would *you* like it," asked Anita, "if every time you tried to tell someone something, someone else butted in and said you were wrong?"

It was a trick question, Ricki knew. She thought carefully before answering. "Oh," she finally said. "You mean—"

"We mean the way you and Vee constantly defend each other," provided Andy. "You two have turned into a couple of lawyers!"

"It's extremely exasperating," said Anita.

"And it's not a requirement for being best friends, you know," said Andy.

"Or for being sisters," Anita added. "In fact, if my sisters, Laura and Marie, and I had tried this kind of stunt on your grandparents, I don't think we'd have gotten past three words."

Andy grinned. "You two have gotten in a lot more than three words."

Ricki couldn't help grinning back. And she wasn't the only one. Vanessa wore a small, half-guilty smile.

"I just hate it when Vee gets yelled at," Ricki said.

"Me, too," added Vanessa. "It's awful when Ricki's being scolded."

Anita shook her head. "Oh, come on. We don't yell and scold. There are things we need to talk about sometimes. We're not monsters about it, are we?"

Ricki shrugged. "Not usually."

"Just unreasonable," said Vanessa.

"Right," agreed Ricki. "Exactly. Unreasonable."

Andy sighed. Grinning at his wife, he said, "You know, I'm not sure you and I knew what we were creating when we turned these two into sisters."

Anita sighed with him. "What a team."

Chapter 8

Vanessa pulled her science book from her locker, put her math book in, and stacked them up neatly, using her lunch sack as a bookend. Next she straightened the Greenpeace calendar taped inside the door.

She liked using her locker. It was her own, small, private part of the school—the one part of the building that she could call her own. The locker was just one of many differences between junior high and intermediate. It was a difference she liked. In fact, Vanessa had to admit there were a lot of things she liked about junior high, now that she'd gotten used to it. For instance, the freedom of flowing from classroom to classroom, instead of sitting in the same one all day. And, because junior high students had to act more responsibly and get to their classes on time, they were treated a little more like adults. At least, that was the theory.

"Vanessa!"

She turned to find Louise Ann rushing down the hall, arms full of books. Her beaded braids danced around her head as she ran. "Have you heard what happened?"

Right behind Louise Ann followed Dani and Randall. Dani's dimples were in full force around her pretty smile. Randall yawned.

"Good news, I suppose," Vanessa said, shutting her locker door.

"About Kimberly!" Louise Ann panted.

Dani, unable to contain herself any longer, cried, "She made it! She made it!"

"Kimberly?" Vanessa's eyebrows shot up. "You mean she made seventh-grade cheerleader?"

"The results are posted on the school office door," reported Louise Ann. "Can you *believe*? Kimberly Morris is a Roosevelt Junior High cheerleader!"

"So is Courtney Haines," added Dani. "She made the other seventh-grade spot."

"Courtney, I can believe. She's been pushing for this since last year," said Vanessa. "But Kimberly—she's so shy!"

Dani shook her head, making her short black hair swing back and forth. "No more."

"The cheerleaders have changed her," said Louise Ann.

"She talks more," Dani explained. "They showed her how to be more outgoing."

Vanessa sighed. "I guess she isn't going to sit with us at lunch anymore."

"Well, she hasn't sat with us for two weeks, during the preliminary practices and tryouts," Louise Ann noted.

"Yet she has not become, oh, how do you say it? Stuck out?" asked Dani.

Randall, apparently just tuning in to the conversation, chuckled and gave Dani a pat on the arm. "You mean stuck *up*."

Dani smiled. "Yes, she is not stuck up. I talked with her. She likes being popular. Oh, there is Ricki."

"Hi, everybody!" Ricki breezed up to them, notebook under one arm and blue jacket slung over the other. "How's it going?"

"We're talking about Kimberly." Louise Ann filled her in. "Isn't it wild?"

Ricki nodded. "Last person you'd expect, right?"

"Right," agreed Louise Ann. "Courtney's been campaigning since intermediate school, but Kimberly . . ."

"Yeah, but Kimberly did work hard for this, you know," Ricki pointed out. "You should have seen her at the practices."

"Oh, yes," said Dani. "You are friends with the cheerleaders, too, Ricki. How exciting! Now we have two cheerleaders from our own old school, Kennedy Intermediate, and a friend who is a friend of the cheerleaders, and—"

Louise Ann rolled her eyes. "Let's not get carried away, okay? Cheerleading is not exactly the top accomplishment of humanity."

Vanessa giggled. Randall joined in with a chuckle. Ricki only grinned a little. True, cheerleading may not be the most useful activity in the world. In fact, it had always seemed pretty dumb to her. But it was cool, in a way, too. Being part of a tight-knit group like that, all best friends, going to the practices and games and parties together. Having everyone look up to you. Being popular wouldn't hurt, either.

On her way to P.E. later that morning, Ricki caught sight of Kimberly, Courtney, and a couple of their fellow squad members stretching out on the playing field beside the gym.

"Hey, Kim!" Ricki called, jogging over to them. "Way to go!"

Kimberly stopped in the middle of a leg lift. "Thanks!" She smiled, so big that both top and bottom rows of braces gleamed.

Ricki stuck out her hand for a shake. "You did it, kid. Congratulations."

A peachy blush tinged Kimberly's cheeks. She was obviously happy as a clam.

"Hey, you, too, Courtney," Ricki added, talking to the other girl.

Brushing a fluff of honey-toned hair away from her eyes, Courtney gave her standard pasted-on smile. "Thanks."

"By the way, Court, how'd you like your pictures? Did they turn out the way you wanted?"

"They were fine," said Courtney.

"That's good." Ricki nodded. "How about everybody else? Did you like your pictures?"

Nicole and Bridgit nodded and grunted something that sounded like, "Yes" in between waist bends. None of them seemed interested in talking, which was a big difference from the last time Ricki had been at a practice. Then, they had all wanted to talk with her about their photos.

"What are you guys up to now, anyway? A practice in the middle of the day?"

Kimberly nodded. "The four of us have our free period now, and the principal said we could use it to get in extra practice time before our first game." Then she giggled. "It's so exciting, Ricki. I—"

"Kimberly, get in formation!" called Bridgit.

Ricki turned to see that all the others had lined up in a triangle, leaving a spot open for Kimberly, who quickly hopped into it.

There was, of course, no spot left open for Ricki. Not that she expected one, but a little conversation wouldn't hurt them, would it? Two weeks ago, when they wanted photos, they had made time for plenty of conversation with her.

If she didn't hurry, she'd be late for P.E. again. She headed for the gym.

On the walkway, she noticed that the two girls ahead of her had identical, waist-length hair. Ricki recognized them from her P.E. class. Inez and Michelle. They always sat together.

Inez's earring glinted in the sunlight as she turned to speak to her friend. A chain of silver filigree, it dangled all the way to her shoulder. Although Ricki couldn't quite hear, she could tell Michelle's answer came in Spanish.

"Callate!"

Ricki knew what that meant. She had heard her Grandma Perla say it a hundred times. *Be quiet!*

" 'Scuse me," Ricki called. "Um, *perdon.*"

The curtain of black hair whirled around. Inez's

earring jiggled. "*Si?* Do you speak Spanish? *Hablas español?*"

Ricki nodded. "*Un poco.* Just a little. Sorry about eavesdropping."

"It's okay." The other girl shrugged. She had long black hair, too, styled almost exactly like Inez's. "We talk too loud sometimes when we think no one can understand us." She wore a long silver earring matching Inez's.

"My grandparents do that, too. They try to use Spanish as a secret code language. I'm Ricki Romero, by the way."

"I'm Michelle Leon, and that's Inez Ibarra."

"Are you two related?"

"Not directly." Inez shook her head. "But people think so because of our hair. We wear the same kind of clothes sometimes, too, because we're both Machas."

"You're what?" Ricki asked.

"Machas. It's kind of a club," Michelle explained.

"We have about fifty female cousins and second cousins and aunts in our family," said Inez, "and we all live in pretty much the same neighborhood and go to the same schools and church, so we decided to make a kind of club."

"It's no big deal, really." Michelle shrugged. "We just wear these earrings. Sometimes at church we all try to sit together, but someone usually comes by to separate us."

"We talk too much," added Inez.

"Our Aunt Patrice has a nail salon where we can meet and talk all we want."

"It's fun," said Inez. "She fixes our nails for free."

"Wow." Ricki grinned. It did sound fun. A whole, huge family of built-in friends, everywhere you went. Instant popularity.

"I guess you have to be in the family to be a Macha, huh?" Ricki asked as they entered the girls' locker room.

Inez shrugged. "No. The word means, oh, something like 'tough' or 'brave.' You know, kind of like 'macho' for men?"

"But you really don't have to be tough or brave to be a Macha," said Michelle. "It's just a name."

"You know Ellen Hemphill?" Inez asked. "She's my friend, so we made her a Macha."

Ricki grinned again. Hmm. Who needed cheerleaders? Here were the Machas instead!

"How do you guys like this hat?" asked Ricki's mother.

She and the girls were at the mall Saturday with Aunt Laura and Suzanne, window shopping.

"You look like a walking fruit basket," said Aunt Laura.

Suzanne laughed. "No! That's a wonderful hat, Anita. Here. You just turn the brim up like so on the side."

"I should have known you'd know what to do with it, Suzanne," Anita said. "Flight attendants always look so chic."

"Oh, really? You should see most of us off the job. Look at the grubbies I'm wearing now, for instance.'' Suzanne pointed at her blue jogging suit and sneakers.

''Are those bananas edible?'' asked Ricki, poking at the array of fruit.

''If you like plastic,'' Vanessa said.

''Too bad.'' Aunt Laura blew upward at a dark brown curl that kept falling over her eye. ''Otherwise this could be a very practical hat. You could just reach up anytime you got hungry and grab a snack.''

''Oh, you're all hopeless.'' Suzanne shook her head. ''You just don't know style when you see it.''

''That's right,'' said Anita. ''It's a gorgeous hat. With a not-so-gorgeous price tag.''

''Yow!'' gasped Aunt Laura, checking out the tag. ''A humongous price tag.''

Anita set the hat back on the head of a mannequin who wore a brightly colored sarong wrapped around in a tiny bikini swimsuit. ''I think only *she* can afford this.''

''Speaking of too expensive.'' Aunt Laura looked at her watch. ''It's about time for that haircut you two talked me into, isn't it?''

''Oh, that's right,'' Anita said. ''Your appointment is at two. And stop complaining. You haven't lived until you've had a style by Monsieur Jules. Besides, today he's thirty percent off.''

''That's my sister, financial advisor, always looking out for me.'' Aunt Laura rolled her brown eyes.

''Well, if it were up to you, my marine biologist sister, you'd only get your hair cut when it got too long to tuck into your scuba wet suit.''

88

"Which would be perfectly sensible." Aunt Laura grinned.

"Do we have to go, too, Mom?" asked Ricki. "Vee and I aren't getting haircuts."

"You two have some sort of pact, don't you?" asked Suzanne. "You always get the same hairstyles together, right?"

Vanessa nodded. "For the past two years. We thought it might help us look like twins."

Ricki made a goofy face. "Clever, aren't we? Anyway, Mom, how about if Vee and I just hang out in the mall. Wouldn't you rather do that, Vee?"

"Definitely," Vanessa agreed. Window shopping was fun, but beauty shops weren't. She hated the smells of the lotions and chemicals.

"By yourselves?" asked Anita.

Ricki sighed. "Yes, by ourselves. The appointment's only for an hour, right? We can meet you back here right at three o'clock."

"All right," Anita finally said. "Right here at three."

The girls watched her and the others rise away on the escalator to the second floor. They all waved.

"Come on," said Ricki. "Want to check out the music videos in juniors?"

Vanessa nodded, and after a moment the two of them stood transmogrified in front of three video screens above the racks of juniors' clothes. On the screens, a man in a blue sequined jumpsuit and a green tricorn pirate's hat climbed up the mast pole of a sailboat, which after a moment turned into a guitar and then into a giant, wriggling snake.

Andy and Anita never let them watch the video channel at home. They accused it of being too violent, too adult, and too weird.

After the girls had spent ten minutes in near-hypnosis in front of the three screens, a saleswoman walked up to them. She wore a red leather minidress, about fourteen metallic bangle bracelets, and no smile.

"Can I help you?" Her tone of voice didn't sound helpful at all. Annoyed was more like it.

"Huh?" asked Ricki, barely taking her eyes off the pirate on the screen.

"Oh. No. Thank you," stammered Vanessa. "We were just— We were just looking." She grabbed her sister's arm and pulled.

"Hey, that was a great song," Ricki complained when they reached the open mall outside the department store. "Why'd you make me leave? I'm going to buy the tape. Is there a record store around here?"

"Yes." Vanessa pointed down the mall. "But the important question is, is there any money around here?"

"I've got two dollars and fifty cents." Rick jiggled a pocketful of change. "Can I borrow some from you?"

"I have exactly one dollar and twenty-nine cents. I don't think that will help."

Ricki sighed. "You know, shopping malls can be pretty boring if you don't have any money. I mean, you just wander around and look at stuff. It's pointless."

"Not really. You can think about things you'd like to get and watch people and—"

"Hey!" Ricki stopped walking and tugged on Vanessa's sleeve.

"What?"

Ricki pointed at a big white sign over one of the shops. It said, NAILS, ETC., in pink curlicue letters.

"That's the Machas' aunt's shop!"

"The who?" Vanessa's left eyebrow went up.

"The Machas. You know, Inez and Michelle. I introduced you to them after school the other day. They have this kind of a club called the Machas, and the nail salon is where they hang out sometimes. Let's go see if they're there."

Vanessa followed reluctantly behind Ricki as they entered the shop. Nail salons didn't smell much better than hair salons.

"May I help you?" asked a large woman with a friendly smile.

"Oh, hi." Ricki smiled back. "I was just wondering, uh— Do you know Inez Ibarra and Michelle Leon?"

The woman smiled twice as wide. "Of course. They're my nieces. Well, second cousins, actually, but you know, in a big family everyone becomes your niece or nephew or aunt or uncle. Do you go to school with them?"

Ricki nodded. "They told me all about the Machas and how they meet here sometimes, so my sister and I thought we'd stop by."

"Oh, the Machas." The woman chuckled, shaking her head. "Those girls are all crazy. They made me join, too. I had to take a solemn oath and everything. Plus I have to wear this whenever they're around. I see them coming, and quick, I pop it on." From a pocket she took a dangly silver earring, just like the ones Michelle and Inez wore. Then she put a finger to her lips. "Don't tell them that Aunt Patrice doesn't wear it all the time, okay?"

Ricki and Vanessa nodded.

"You're not wearing your earrings, either, I see," Patrice pointed out.

"Well, we're not—" Ricki began.

"Oh, I see," Patrice interrupted. Hands in the pockets of her smock, she peered at Ricki's ears, then at Vanessa's. "Your ears aren't pierced. A little timid?"

"Timid?" Vanessa repeated, thinking, *No, not timid. Terrified.* She'd no sooner get her ears pierced than get her nose tattooed.

"No, we're not timid," said Ricki. "Not a bit.'

Vanessa stared at her, mouth open.

"Well, then." Patrice gestured at a small pink sign over the cash register that read,

Earpiercing here! Wear those beautiful baubles you always dreamed of. Only $25!

"We don't have twenty-five dollars," said Vanessa, relieved. For a moment it had seemed that Ricki was actually considering the offer.

"I have a credit card," said Ricki, not adding that her mother had given it to her to use only in an emergency.

Vanessa chewed busily on the inside of her cheek while Patrice rang up a customer's purchase of nail polish. One look at Ricki told Vanessa all she needed to know. Ricki was completely serious about this ear piercing thing—for both of them!

Patrice came back. "We'll need your parents' permission. Why don't you come in tomorrow with your mother or father?"

"They can't come," Ricki said quietly.

"They can't? Why not?" asked Patrice.

"Well . . ."

Vanessa saw Ricki swallow and lower her eyes sadly.

"They're . . . My father's dead."

Patrice's face turned pale.

Vanessa locked her eyes on Ricki, mouth hanging open. She could barely believe what she'd heard. True, Ricki's father died when Ricki was three years old. But Vanessa knew exactly what Ricki was trying to accomplish with that fact, and she didn't like it.

"Oh, honey, I'm sorry." Patrice frowned. "Well, are you sure that your mother can't—"

Ricki shook her head. "Mom works so hard. She can't come shopping with me very often, so . . ."

That part was true, too, Vanessa thought. Still, Ricki was stretching things awfully far.

"Oh." Patrice's eyes glistened, and her chin went a little weak. She patted Ricki's arm. "Okay, honey. Why don't you go sit down? I'll be there in a few minutes."

"Come on, Vee." Ricki motioned to her.

Vanessa didn't move a muscle.

"Hey, won't it be great to wear earrings?" Ricki whispered. She had a kind of a glazed look in her eyes, the kind she always got when she was trying to get Vanessa to do something Vanessa knew she'd regret later.

"Ricki, how could you say those things?" Vanessa whispered.

"Oh, Vee. Don't be such a stick in the mud. I didn't lie. Anyway, everyone says ear piercing doesn't hurt. Come on."

"They put *needles* through your *earlobes,* Ricki. How can it not hurt?" Vanessa cringed. "Besides, what do I want holes in my ears for?"

"For earrings, Vee. You want holes in your ears for earrings."

At that moment Patrice came back and ushered them to two big, pink, fluffy-looking chairs. They felt fluffy, too. Vanessa sank into one. She felt she might keep sinking and eventually disappear, which might not be a bad idea at that particular moment. It had been a long time since she'd seen Ricki so determined about anything.

Patrice pulled a brown leather box from a drawer. "All right. Are we ready? Who would like to go first?"

Ricki pointed at Vanessa. "She would."

"Me?" Vanessa shrank away.

"Okay, okay." Ricki sighed. "Be chicken. I'll go first." She shut her eyes. "Go ahead."

Vanessa shut her eyes, too. She didn't open them, not even a couple of minutes later when she heard Ricki squeal. Just listening made her heart race, so she tried humming to herself to drown out the sounds of Patrice's instruments clinking against each other.

In a moment she felt a pat on her hand. She jumped
half a foot. Her eyes flew open.

Patrice smiled at her. "It's only me, dear. I just
wanted to let you know it's over. Look at your
friend."

Ricki's eyes glistened as if she'd cried a little. But
she held her chin high, alternately grinning at
Vanessa and admiring her reddened earlobes in
Patrice's pink tabletop mirror.

"Nice, eh?" asked Patrice.

Vanessa stared worriedly at the instruments. "Yes,
but—"

"I know. You're not ready, are you?" Patrice patted her hand again. "Some other time."

"You're not going to do it?" Ricki demanded.

"I don't want to," said Vanessa.

Ricki frowned. "But you— I did it."

"Now, now," said Patrice. "Sisters don't have to
do everything together, you know. One day, Ricki.
Maybe another day, your sister. Now leave those gold
posts in for six weeks, all right? Twist them around
twice a day, and apply this antiseptic lotion daily,
too."

Rick nodded. "Thank you, Ms.—"

"Oh, call me Patrice, honey." Her smile at Ricki
was sad. She looked embarrassed when Ricki gave
her the credit card, as if she really didn't want to
charge her.

Vanessa crossed her fingers, hoping that Ricki
wouldn't go any farther with her sob story.

"Come back to visit, okay?" Patrice said as they
left the store.

"Okay," answered Ricki. That was the last word she said all the way back to the department store.

"Are you mad at me?" Vanessa asked. "You have no right to be, you know. It's my right to keep my ears the way they are."

"Great," said Ricki. "Fine. Be that way. Just how you always are. Never willing to try something new. Always turning your nose up at things *I* want to do. You didn't have to act like you were going to go along with it if—"

"I didn't! I just—"

"Ricki! Vanessa! Hi!" It was Ricki's mother, hurrying toward them with Suzanne. "Aunt Laura's going to be a while longer with Monsieur Jules, so Suzanne and I came to look at the shoes. Are you having f—" She halted midsentence to squint at her daughter.

Vanessa held her breath. She hadn't thought ahead to this part.

Neither had Ricki.

Chapter 9

"Hon, where'd you get the earrings?" asked Anita.

Ricki grinned. "Like them? The aunt of some friends of ours has a nail shop down the—"

"Ricki, are those *pierced* earrings?"

Still grinning, Ricki nodded.

The dusky brown of Anita's eyes went several shades darker. She took a deep breath and let it out slowly. Then she looked at Vanessa and Suzanne. "Will you excuse us for a moment?"

Vanessa opened her mouth, then shut it. Half of her wanted to step in and explain things to Anita. The ear piercing was a spur of the moment thing. Ricki didn't mean to be so impulsive. She just was.

Vanessa's other half took one look at Anita's glowering eyes and didn't dare say a word. That half won.

It wasn't fair. It just wasn't. Slouching on her bed Sunday afternoon, Ricki tossed her softball into the air over and over, seeing how close she could get to the ceiling without hitting it. That was the most excitement she was likely to have anytime soon. For two weeks, to be exact. That was how long she had been grounded for.

Two weeks. No phone privileges. No going to movies, no going anywhere. Except school, soccer practice, and the dentist next Wednesday. Mom said she could go to Mill Pond Park, too, but that was only a photography class field trip for nature close-ups.

How come getting her ears pierced was such a crime? She hadn't robbed a bank or anything. The way her mom was acting, though, she may as well have.

"This is serious," Anita had said quietly yesterday afternoon in the shoe department. "I get the feeling that you're testing me, Ricki."

Ricki's earlobes had begun to itch. She was trying desperately not to rub them. "Testing you?"

"You want to see how far you can push the limit with me, I think. Well, this is it. You have definitely hit it."

"But Mom, all I did was—"

"All you did was something you knew I wouldn't want you to do. We talked about this kind of thing just last week, and I said you may not wear makeup until—"

"This isn't makeup. It's earrings." Ricki tried not to whine. It was so frustrating.

"How did you pay for it, anyway?" her mother asked.

"Um, well, remember the credit card?"

Mom looked furious. "For emergencies."

"Yeah, that one. Well . . ."

"You're grounded. Two weeks."

"Two weeks!"

"What you did was childish. You must have known that if I disapproved of makeup, I wouldn't want you to pierce your ears, either."

"You never said so."

"Certainly you don't expect me to give you a printed list, do you?" Mom stuck a hand on her hip.

Ricki shrugged. "I just didn't think about it."

"Honey, you're a very smart girl. You *need* to think about things. Don't just jump in and do something the minute it occurs to you. You must have had doubts. I wish we could have talked about it first."

"Why? You'd have said no anyway."

"That's true. I would have." Mom nodded.

"Then what's the point?"

"The point is that I'm your mother, Ricki. And you're twelve years old."

"But these are *my* ears, no matter what age I am."

Mom didn't seem to care whose ears they were. "Two weeks, Ricki. We'll talk more about this later, at home."

Ricki knew from the bright spots of color on her mother's high cheekbones that there was no use in trying to change her mind. The water would only get hotter.

So far her mom hadn't brought up the subject again at home. Things had been going pretty normally around the house. Except for being grounded. Whenever the phone rang for Ricki, the caller was told that Ricki couldn't come to the phone that week. It was ridiculous. Also, Ricki's ears itched. Patrice had said

99

they might for a day or two. At dinner, she had wanted to scratch. Of course, she didn't. Her mom would have noticed. Ricki refused to give her that satisfaction.

Ricki tossed her softball high. This was no fun. For the first time in her life, she felt as if she and her mom were playing a game of tackle football—on opposing teams.

"What is *that*?" asked Vanessa's father, pointing at the poster she had just hung over her desk.

"It's from Oceans Guard, the anti-whaling group. Did you know that every year thousands of whales are killed—even the ones that are protected by law?"

"No, I didn't. That's pretty awful." Andy winced. "But can you really stand to look at that poster all the time, Vee? The picture is, well, gruesome."

"That's exactly how a whale looks when it's being slaughtered, Dad. If we don't keep it in mind, we won't do anything about it."

"Well, you know, I try to do something about it sometimes. I've stuffed envelopes for anti-war groups and signed petitions for clean air. But I don't keep a picture of a bleeding whale over my desk."

"Would you like one?" Vanessa searched in her desk drawer. "I have another here somewhere."

"No, no, thanks. That's not what—I was just trying to say that—Oh, well. Never mind. I came to ask what kind of pizza you'd like. We're ordering in."

"Pizza?" Vanessa adored pizza. But her face fell.

She couldn't have pizza. Not anymore. Never again. "I don't want any, thanks."

"Huh? No pizza? Come on, Vee. You must be kidding. You love—"

"I can't, Dad," Vanessa said, envisioning the cows lined up in narrow stalls at inhumane dairy farms.

"Wait a minute. Does this have something to do with this vegetarian kick you're on?"

Vanessa frowned. Why didn't anyone understand her? "It's not a 'kick,' Dad. I can't consume animal products."

Andy crossed his arms. "Then what *will* you eat tonight?"

"I'll find something."

Andy sighed and finally said, "All right."

Vanessa knew he didn't mean it. She knew it was not all right with him that she had become a vegetarian.

He left without another word. Dad didn't understand. Nobody did. People just went on eating meat right and left. Nobody cared.

Not even Clem. Clem said she'd never give meat up, no matter which pack of nuts happened to hoist up the vegetarian flag next. She said she was too old to be at the whim of the latest craze. Yet Clem was a person who really loved animals, who devoted all her time to them. Imagine people who *didn't* love animals. And all those people who even abused them!

Vanessa gazed up at her whale kill poster, and then at her veal calf poster, and then at the one with the

Dalmatian mother and the little pups who might never find a home. Her eyes stung with tears. She sniffled.

At that moment she wished more than anything that she could talk with Ricki. Ricki always understood. At least, she *used* to. These days, Ricki wasn't even paying attention. She looked bored whenever Vanessa tried to explain to her about animal rights. Of course, Ricki did have other things on her mind—being grounded, having holes in her ears. But she hardly even answered whenever Vanessa tried to cheer her up. All she did was mope and complain about not getting to talk on the phone with her other friends.

Two weeks ago, she and Ricki were still best friends and sisters, sharing things, defending each other against their parents. Now things were totally different.

Vanessa took her cello from its case, dragged the bow across the strings a couple of times, then put it away. She didn't really feel like practicing. In fact, she hadn't felt like practicing at all these past few days. Next she sat down to do her homework, but midway through a math problem she got a funny feeling in her stomach—one she had been getting a lot lately. A gnawing, raw feeling.

After a few minutes, the doorbell rang. Vanessa heard her dad talking to the pizza man. The feeling in her stomach got worse as the aroma of fresh pizza drifted up the stairs. Or maybe Vanessa only imagined the smell. She could see the steamy layers of cheese and sausage and taste the tangy tomato sauce. It seemed like years since she'd had pizza or anything besides salads and apples.

Gazing at the veal calf for strength, she promised, "No, I won't."

"Sure you don't want some of my ham sandwich?" Louise Ann asked Vanessa Monday at lunch.
"Please stop trying to tempt me, Louise Ann."
"Hey, I'm not. Honest. I just feel sorry for you."
"Me, too," said Randall. "I mean, not eating meat? That would drive me up a tree."
Lately, Randall had started to relax and talk more at the lunch table. Vanessa wished that today he'd go back to being quiet.
"Cheese, I love the most," said Dani. "No more cheese would be awful."
"Wait, everybody. Let's not make the girl feel worse, okay?" suggested Louise Ann.
Vanessa smiled gratefully. Sometimes, she felt that Louise Ann understood her better than anyone. Or, at least, she *tried* to understand. Which was more than anyone else did these days.
Vanessa stole a glance across the room at Ricki, who sat with Michelle and Inez. She had started sitting there yesterday, stopping by the old table first to ask if anyone wanted to join them. Vanessa felt so surprised she couldn't answer. Louise Ann and Dani had said no, thanks. And that was that.
It shouldn't have been surprising, Vanessa decided. For weeks, it seemed she and Ricki had been drifting in opposite directions. Now, there was no doubt they were on completely different courses.
"I think it's good you are trying to be a vegetarian and help the animals," said Dani. "I love animals."

Louise Ann nodded. "It's great when people do something they believe in."

"I'm not doing much," said Vanessa. "And if Clementine's wildlife rehab center closes down, I'll hardly be able to do anything."

Louise Ann frowned. "Why should it close down?"

Vanessa explained it all to them. Her friends were horrified. Even Randall, who usually did his best to appear bored, looked mildly concerned.

"That's awful," said Dani.

"There's got to be some extra money somewhere in the government to help her," added Louise Ann.

"Yeah, my dad always complains about the tax money he has to pay not going to the right causes," Randall said. "How come that money can't be spent on good things?"

"I'm sure a lot of people would want to donate to the rehab center, if they knew about it," suggested Louise Ann.

Vanessa stopped in the middle of a bite of salad. "Wait. That's it!"

"That's what?"

"That's what I can do. I've been trying to think of some way to help Clementine keep the center going. Maybe more people need to know about it. I mean, to begin with, right here at school."

"Hey, I've got it!" said Louise Ann. "Easy! Dani, you're in the school Service Club, aren't you?"

"Oh, yes. I joined. It's my first club in the United States. At our next meeting we're going to talk about our projects for the year. We will have bake sales, dances, bowling marathons, and other things to raise money for charity projects. Perhaps the center for animals could become one of the projects.''

"Just what I had in mind!'' said Louise Ann.

"Do you really think so?'' Vanessa brightened.

"Our meeting is next Wednesday,'' said Dani. "I will tell them about the center for animals. I think it might be a popular project!''

Chapter 10

"Rats," Ricki muttered under her breath, erasing the last half of the math equation she had just written in her notebook. She realized she had copied half of problem one and half of problem two from the text-book. It looked like one of the weird imaginary animals made with those kids' zoological puzzle pieces. Half monkey, half giraffe.

Come to think of it, that was how most math problems looked to her anyway.

"Got any colored markers?" asked the girl next to her, Dale Lanting.

Ricki handed her a green felt tip.

The two of them sat at a table in the library Friday afternoon, working together. Everybody in Mrs. Minsk's class had been assigned partners for a special project.

"Well," said Dale, leaning back. "Think of anything for this problem?" One of her arms dangled over the back of her chair. It was the arm that had a sleeve. The other arm didn't have a sleeve. Her jacket sleeve had been torn off at the shoulder, on purpose. Under it she wore a Peter Gabriel T-shirt, because she was really into rock music. Dale was a very unusual person. Her auburn hair was unusual, too, shorn close to her head all over, like a boy's buzz. Except she wore a huge yellow polka-dot bow right over her left ear.

"I don't really get what we're supposed to do," said Ricki. "Turn these equations into word problems? '12 + 12x = 36.' How do we do that?"

Dale flipped the cap off the marker. "Like this. Here's a birthday party." She drew a table and chairs and twelve balloons on a page in her notebook.

"Hey, that's good," said Ricki. "You can draw."

"I like to. Anyway, let's say you started with three gallons of ice cream at your birthday party. Three gallons at twelve scoops per gallon. That's what the number 36 is for, right?"

"Oh," said Ricki. "What's the first '12' for?"

"Well, let's say it's how many scoops of ice cream have disappeared. And let's say you want to divide what's left equally. That's what the '12x' is for."

Ricki frowned. The equation still made little sense to her, but it was fun to watch Dale draw a tub of chocolate ice cream and plates of cake. She wished she could draw, too, besides look as interesting and unusual as Dale.

"Your friends are real pigs, okay?" Dale grinned. "And you want to keep them from fighting. So you want to give them all the same amount of ice cream out of what remains."

"Hmm." A tiny, dim light flickered in Ricki's head. "So 12 + 12x is the total amount of ice cream we're all going to eat."

"Right. You're already down twelve scoops, and

the 'x' stands for how many more scoops you can give each person from what's left."

"Two scoops each. Oh, wow!" Ricki whispered. The light grew brighter, shining on the idea of word problems.

"Understand now?"

"Yeah, I think so!" Ricki felt like jumping up and down. She was beginning to get it.

"Want to try number two?" asked Dale.

Ricki looked at the problem. "Looks like the same kind of thing, right? Except it's got 'y's instead of 'x's."

Dale nodded, repinning the bow over her ear.

Ricki picked up the marking pen. "I don't know how to draw. I'll just write it out, like a story."

A girl had forty-two hair bows, Ricki wrote on a fresh sheet of paper. *And seven friends.*

Dale giggled. "That's good." She kept giggling as Ricki's story about a girl whose friends fought over her hair bows got funnier and sillier.

Ricki giggled, too, happy that word problems and equations finally made some sense. *And* she had a new friend!

"Dad?" Vanessa called as she got home Monday. "Hi, Kirby!"

The dog bounded up, tail wagging a mile a minute. Then his ears went up. He aimed his big black nose at the shoe box in Vanessa's arms.

"No, Kirby." Vanessa shook her head. "Sorry. This is not for you."

"Cheep! Cheep!" came cries from the box.

Kirby's eyes widened.

"Baby birds," she whispered, and held the box up high, just in case he got any ideas about them. "Dad? Where are you?"

"Not here," called a voice from the dining room. "Said to tell you he'd be back in a few."

"Is that you, Bernard?" asked Vanessa.

"Yup," he answered when she reached the dining room. He kneeled in front of a pink wooden shape, wiping it with a cloth. "Your dad had to rush to the post office. Said he'll be right back. How're you?"

"Fine, thanks. How are—?" She stopped midsentence, staring at the sculpture. "What is that?"

Bernard grinned. "Different, huh? Not my usual. For two years I do totem poles. Now, this." He scratched his bald head and adjusted his glasses.

"It's— It's an *arm*, Bernard."

"Really? Does it really look like one? Great!" He ran the cloth over it again. "Been shaping it all day."

Vanessa frowned. "Why are you making an arm?"

"Hey, it's almost Halloween. A radio station down in San Jose is putting on a masked ball. Hired me to make some props. Not bad, eh? Here, look."

Vanessa gingerly poked a finger at the arm. "Eeuu! How disgusting!"

Bernard grinned happily. Then he peered into Vanessa's shoe box. "Hey, where'd you get those?"

"They're hummingbird chicks. They were born really late in the season. I volunteer at a wildlife rehabilitation center down the street. The woman who runs it hasn't had much rest lately, so I offered to

109

take the chicks for the night. They have to be fed every twenty minutes.''

''Fun.'' Bernard made chirping sounds at the birds. ''Hi, guys.''

''Well, I'd better get started. Good luck with the arm.''

''A leg, too,'' said Bernard. ''Got to do that next.''

Heading upstairs, Vanessa decided that thinking about the arm and leg was almost gross enough to distract her from what her dad would say about the birds.

He wasn't going to like it. Neither would Anita. Already, Kirby was complaining. She shut her bedroom door and left him in the hall, whining.

''Sorry, boy,'' she told him through the door. Baby birds might be just too tempting for him. They looked and sounded an awful lot like his squeaky toys.

From her backpack, Vanessa took out the eyedropper and the jar of feed formula Clementine had given her. ''Okay, sweeties. Who's first?''

All three of the chicks chirped up at her with wide-open beaks, craning their wobbly necks as high as they could.

Vanessa chose the smallest one. Like its brothers and sisters, it seemed like nothing but a puff of down. Cradling it against her chest, she could feel the racing beat of its tiny heart.

Gently, Vanessa slipped the eyedropper tube down the chick's throat. The chick gulped and flapped its tiny wings. After squirting in the formula, Vanessa slipped the tube out and settled the bird into a napkin-lined strawberry basket in a corner of the shoe box, taking one of its nestmates out next.

Sticking eyedroppers down baby birds' gullets hadn't always seemed so easy, Vanessa remembered. The first time, she had been terrified of hurting the little creature, even though Clementine had explained that mother birds used their beaks exactly the same way. Now, after hundreds of feedings, it finally felt natural to her. The difference, though, between this brood of chicks and the dozens of others she had fed at Clem's was that these weren't at Clem's. They were in her own room.

As she fed the second bird, Vanessa heard the front door open and shut. Her dad was home.

She put the chick in the strawberry basket with the first one, then took a deep breath.

"Time to tell him about you guys," she whispered.

On her way downstairs, the phone rang. It couldn't be for Ricki, because by now all Ricki's friends knew she couldn't take phone calls until her grounding period was over.

"Vee!" Andy called from the living room doorway.

"Yes?"

"Oh, there you are. Hi, Rainbow. Phone for you."

"Really?" She jogged down the last few stairs, Kirby at her heels, and picked it up in the hall. "Hello?"

"Hello, this is Dani. How are you? I have news."

"Oh, about the Service Club meeting?"

"Yes. It was this afternoon. I just got home." Dani paused. "I wanted to tell you right away."

111

"Oh, no. You don't sound happy."

"I'm sorry, Vanessa. The club did not vote to make the wildlife center one of our charity projects. Not interesting enough, they said."

"Not interesting? You're kidding! Animals are *very* interesting."

Dani sighed. "I believe so, too. But the others . . . they don't think so."

"That's the problem. Nobody's interested in animals. Nobody cares."

"I'm sorry, Vanessa. I tried—"

"I know you did, Dani," Vanessa reassured her friend. "Thanks. It was really nice of you. I just wish I knew some way to—"

"Cheep! Cheep!"

"Oh, gosh," said Vanessa. "I have to go, Dani." The two chicks she hadn't fed yet were complaining.

"Cheep! Cheep!"

"Is everything all right?" Dani asked.

"Yes, but—"

"Vee?" Andy appeared in the living room doorway. "Did you hear something?"

"Um, good-bye, Dani. See you tomorrow." She hung up. "Something like what, Dad?"

"Well . . . birds, I think. Baby birds."

Vanessa nodded.

"Wow." Andy shook his head. "First ghosts, then raccoons, now baby birds. Boy, is this house popular!"

"Dad—" Vanessa began.

"They can't be in the crawl space." Andy stared

toward the attic in thought. "I sealed it. The window up there is shut. So where could they—"

"Dad."

He finally looked at her. "Hmm?"

"They're in my room."

"Cheep! Cheep!"

"In your room?" Andy's brown eyes widened.

"In a box." Vanessa confessed. "They're— they're babies."

Slowly, her dad began to nod. "Oh. I get it. Let me guess. From Clem's."

Vanessa nodded again.

"You didn't ask me about this, Vanessa."

"I know. I was going to, but you weren't here."

Andy sighed. "The one day I'm gone for half an hour, you pick to bring home a nest."

"It's only for one night. Clem's got her hands full, and they have to be fed every twenty minutes, dawn to dusk."

"You're going to feed them every twenty minutes? When," Andy asked, "are you going to get your homework done, Vee? And practice your cello? And *sleep*, for heaven's sake?"

"Just one night, Dad. Not forever. I'll get everything done."

Another chorus of chirps cascaded down the stairs.

"Maybe you will," he said, "but you won't be worth much at school tomorrow, will you?"

Still, Vanessa felt hopeful. Her dad hadn't said no. He wasn't happy, but he wasn't angry, either.

"Tonight," he said. "One night, Vee. But not again, all right?"

113

She smiled. "Just one night."

"However," her dad went on, "tomorrow I want you to take the birds back to Clementine's and let her know you're cutting back on your hours there."

"But Dad, I already cut back! You made me stop going every day."

"Two afternoons per week, Vee."

"*Two?* Dad, that's not—"

"This is not up for negotiation."

"But, Dad—"

"Cheep!"

Andy shook his head. "I've got to get back to work now. And so, apparently, do you." He ambled off to the living room.

"Cheep!"

Vanessa stared after him, chewing on her cheek. This wasn't fair. It wasn't fair at all.

Chapter 11

"I'm sick of my hair," said Ricki, aiming her portable drier at a big, wet clump of it after P.E. Monday.

A line of other girls stood in front of the locker room mirrors along with her, drying their own manes. Michelle and Inez stood next to Ricki. Alison was at the far end. Dale sat on a bench tying her shoes. She had already dried her short buzz with just a couple of flicks of a towel.

"Must be great to have it short." Ricki sighed.

Dale nodded. "It's pretty easy." She got up and stood beside Ricki to pin a blue bow over her ear.

"When did you cut it?" asked Ricki.

"Last year. It was already short. I just asked them to cut an extra inch off."

"Didn't anybody complain? Your mom or dad?"

Dale shrugged. "Mom's hair is short, too. Dad's is long, down to his shoulders. He wears it in a ponytail to keep it out of the way at work. He repairs telephone lines, up on the poles."

"Your dad gets to climb those poles? Cool!" said Ricki. "My stepdad's hair is kind of long, too. He's a rock musician."

"*That's* cool." Dale grinned.

"Is your mom's hair as short as yours?" Ricki asked.

"No." Dale ran a hand over her hair to ruffle it. "It was, almost, but now she's got a job in an insurance office, so she has to look more . . ."

"Boring?"

Dale smiled. "Right. But she decided to be only half boring. She left half of it short and grew the other half long."

"You're kidding!" Ricki grabbed a handful of hair on the right side of her head and folded it up under itself. "Like this?"

"Kind of." Dale pushed the short half shorter, to just above Ricki's ear, then folded the rest in a downward wedge to the other side, just below her ear.

"Hey, this looks cool," said Ricki. "Kind of like a roller coaster swooping down from one ear to the other."

Dale nodded.

Ricki turned her head from side to side to examine herself in the mirror. "Got any scissors?"

"What do you mean?" Dale blinked blue eyes.

"Scissors," repeated Ricki, still looking at herself. She stuck out her lips in a pout, the way models did in magazines. "You know, to cut with."

Dale asked, "You want to cut your hair?"

"I want *you* to cut it for me," Ricki said, "like your mom's."

"Now?"

Ricki shrugged. "Why not? I'm sick of my hair. It's always been long. I have to braid it or tie it back to get it out of the way. Hey, Alison!'' she called. "Do you still have those scissors in your art kit?''

From the other end of the mirror, Alison called back, "Want them?''

"Yeah. I'm going to cut my hair.''

Almost every head in the locker room turned.

"Now?'' asked Michelle.

"There are only ten minutes before next period,'' Inez pointed out.

Alison rummaged in her book bag and brought out the scissors.

Dale asked, "Do you really want a haircut, Ricki?''

Ricki looked in the mirror. She saw the eyes of the other girls fixed on her. She saw her own black, determined eyes. And then, she imagined seeing another pair of eyes—green, angry. Blond eyebrows, frowning.

They had a pact. She and Vanessa had vowed to keep their hair the same length, same style. It was the closest they'd ever get to looking like twins. But that promise was made three years ago, Ricki told herself. Elementary school. This was junior high! Goofy kid promises didn't hold anymore.

Besides, she and Vanessa were sisters and best friends, not clones, right?

"Yeah, I want you to cut it,'' she told Dale. "Hurry.'' *Before I change my mind*, she thought.

Dale shrugged. "Okay.'' She took the scissors from Alison and lifted a wet shock of Ricki's hair. "Ready?''

Ricki nodded.

Off went the hair.

Some of it landed on Ricki's shoulder, the rest on the floor. Ricki looked down at it. Her thumb hurt. She realized she had bitten the nail halfway off.

"Well, that was the worst part." Inez sighed, patting Ricki's arm. "The first snip. It won't be so bad now."

"Hold still, Ricki," Dale said. "Keep your head down, okay?" She chose another section of hair, combed it, and snipped.

No one moved. All the girls watched in fascination. Dale took a few final snips, wiped her hands on a towel, and handed the scissors back to Alison.

"That's it?" asked Inez.

Ricki looked in the mirror.

Michelle pointed at the right side of Ricki's head. "It's longer on this side."

"I know." Dale nodded. "It's supposed to be."

"Oh," said Michelle.

Inez nodded, "Oh."

All the others kept quiet.

For a moment, Ricki just stared at herself. Then she shook her head hard, like Kirby. As she shook, her hair spun out in the shape of a warped Frisbee. Water droplets sprayed in all directions. When she stopped, the hair fell back into place in a kind of a lopsided black bonnet.

She laughed. "Hey, this is cool!"

"One side's longer than the other!" Jeremy Howard pointed and laughed at Ricki in the car pool after soccer that afternoon.

118

"Jeremy, stop yelling." Wincing, Mr. Howard held his head in one hand and gripped the steering wheel with the other. Mr. Howard never had much patience.

Ricki was losing hers, too. After the game, she and everyone else had piled quickly into their cars. The weather was so windy and drizzly that they all played in knit caps and rain jackets. Until she pulled her cap off in the car, no one had noticed her haircut. Then the wisecracks started.

"Why'd you whack off your braids?" Lester Washington asked.

"Tired of 'em," Ricki replied.

"Hey, I know. She leaned her head too far to the right and it hit a chain saw," Jeremy theorized.

"Quiet! Now!" Mr. Howard ordered. "One more wise guy and the lot of you get out to walk. You included, Jeremy!"

By the time they got to Ricki's house, the boys had kept themselves quiet long enough to let her think out a plan. A grand entrance. That would be the best way to introduce her new look to the family.

The house seemed empty. Lately her mom had been on a savings kick and roamed the house turning lights off, even if you happened to be in the room. Annoying. But now it was good. Maybe if she ran upstairs fast enough, they wouldn't see her. Her mom and Andy were probably in the kitchen and Vanessa in her room. Finally, Ricki made it to her own room and shut the door.

Ten minutes later she wore her headphone cassette player turned up to a Morris Boris tape, a tie-dyed

T-shirt borrowed from Dale, and a string of beads that spelled PEACE (also borrowed from Dale). Over that came her oldest sweat jacket carefully torn at the shoulder, the collar, and the elbow. Perfect.

Humming, Ricki skipped downstairs and into the dining room. Voices drifted from the kitchen. She couldn't wait to see their faces when they got a load of her hair. What a kick!

"Rats!" she muttered, rubbing her knee, which she had just banged on a chair. If everything weren't so darn dark! After fumbling along the wall for the light switch, Ricki flipped it on.

She started humming again, heading for the kitchen. Then she froze, unable to move. "Yahhhh!" she shrieked.

An arm dangled from the chandelier. And a leg— a whole leg with a knee and a foot and toes—lay on the table like a centerpiece.

Ricki's heart raced. Her mouth went dry. She wanted to run but was paralyzed with horror.

Suddenly the kitchen door flew open. Ricki whirled around. It was her mother.

"Mom!" Ricki pointed at the arm and the leg.

But her mother was already gasping, "Oh, my god!" She pointed at Ricki. "What have you done?"

"The arm, the leg—" Ricki panted.

"Those are Bernard's, Ricki."

"Bernard's arm and leg?" Ricki stared at her mother. Then something occurred to her. She peered at the arm. It was very pink and healthy looking. Carefully, with one finger, she felt it. "It's wood, Mom. And it has no fingernails."

"I told you, they're Bernard's. But your hair, Ricki . . ."

Ricki scrunched up her nose. "My hair?" She reached for her braids, then remembered. "Oh. My hair. Yeah."

"Honey, what have you done?"

"To my hair? I cut it."

"That's fairly obvious."

Andy came in from the kitchen, wiping his hands on a towel. "Hi, Ricki. I guess you noticed Bernard's pieces. Oh, and you cut your hair."

"Those *pieces* nearly killed me!" Ricki clutched at her heart. "I nearly passed out!"

Andy grinned sheepishly. "Sorry about that. But it *is* almost Halloween, you know. Everyone needs a good scare for the occasion."

"Ricki?" The voice came from behind her. It was Vanessa's voice and made Ricki's stomach feel queasy. The other shoe, as they say, was about to drop.

Slowly, Ricki turned.

Vanessa didn't say a word. For a moment she just stared. Then she took a deep breath as if she might speak to Ricki. But she didn't. Not a word the rest of the evening.

Ricki couldn't understand what Vanessa was so steamed about. It was as if she had cut off her nose or her head—not just her hair! What was the big deal?

During dinner, no one talked about the haircut. Mom bugged her about her headphone cassette player, saying that the dinner table was not the place for it. Ricki thought the dinner table that night happened to be the perfect place for it, but she turned it off, leaving the headphones on.

To her mother, that was the last straw.

"We need to talk," said Anita after they had all cleaned up the kitchen. "You and me."

Half a minute later they sat in the den, doors shut.

Ricki held her breath. A private powwow meant serious business.

"I think," said her mother, "I haven't been fair to you."

Ricki perked up. "You haven't?"

Mom shook her head. "Not at all. I've been looking at individual incidents and actions, instead of at the whole picture."

"Which whole picture?" Maybe this wasn't as good as it had sounded, Ricki decided.

"*Your* whole picture, honey. What's been going on for you this semester. Actually this whole year. There have been quite a few changes in our lives."

Ricki nodded. "But not bad changes."

Anita smiled. "No, not bad changes." She took Ricki's hand. "You're happy with how things have worked out, aren't you? Our new family?"

"It's great," said Ricki, not adding her suspicion that at the moment, her sister detested her.

"I think it's great, too," her mom agreed. "Still, any kind of change can be, well, disruptive. And we've had our share recently. Junior high is a big change. You've had some adjusting to do, haven't you? A new school, new routine, new friends . . ."

Ricki shrugged. "I like it." She still felt anxious. What was Mom getting at?

"Junior high is a time when people often start trying on new ideas, new attitudes, new ways of looking at themselves."

"Mom, you sound like one of those experts they have on 'Oprah.' "

Anita laughed. "What I'm trying to say, hon, is that I was getting awfully angry with you, until I realized something."

"What?"

"Well, wearing makeup, piercing your ears, dressing differently, and now this . . . unique hairstyle . . . I was taking it too personally." Anita's brown eyes gazed into Vanessa's aquarium along the wall. "It seemed you were aiming those changes at me, to prove that you could defy my wishes, or shock me, or who knows what. But now . . . well, Andy suggested I think about my own junior high and high school years. And I did. I remember wanting desperately to fit in. The problem was I didn't know who to fit in *as*. So for a while I tried on different personalities, attitudes, clothes, hairstyles. I do remember how it felt, honey."

Ricki squinted at her mother. This really was like "Oprah." She could just see it. Anita in front of the camera. *Yes*, she'd say, *my child was one of those. A Junior High Chameleon. Changing every day. It was a living nightmare.*

"Mom, do you really think that's what I'm doing?"

Her mother shrugged. "Maybe."

"Well, at least you're not ticked off about my hair."

"I'm not exactly delighted by it." Mom shrugged. "Any more than I was about your ear piercing. But at least the haircut isn't permanent."

"You're going to make me grow it out?"

Mom shook her had. "No. I'm not going to make you grow it out. It is *your* hair, after all."

"Then how come you got so mad when I said these are my ears?"

Her mom sighed in exasperation. "Are *you* always logical and rational? I don't know. Ear piercing is more emotional than haircutting. And it *is* something you should have talked with me about. I did get angry, and rightly so." She sighed again. "I have a sneaking feeling that the two of us are going to be doing a lot of that in the coming years—getting angry with each other."

A weird, sinking feeling hit Ricki's stomach. It was as if her mom was saying good-bye to her daughter's childhood or something.

"Mom, I—" Ricki's voice caught. Her throat and her eyes started to sting. It occurred to her that she might cry. But she hardly ever cried. She wasn't like Vanessa, who cried at the drop of a hat. What was happening to her?

What kept going through her head was that someday—someday soon—she and her mom wouldn't mean the same things to each other anymore. Ricki was supposed to grow up. That's what Anita had been talking about. Growing up. Changing. She—Ricki—becoming different.

124

She wasn't sure she wanted to be different. She liked herself the way she was.

Without a word, Anita took Ricki in her arms and held her close. She stroked Ricki's hair, the short side.

Ricki felt about five years old again. It was embarrassing—sniffing up tears in her mommy's lap. At the same time, though, she felt twenty-five.

Maybe that was the hard part about being twelve. Being stuck in the middle.

Chapter 12

Beef tamales. Cheese enchiladas. Chicken tacos.

Vanessa's nostrils filled with the aroma of the Mexican buffet laid out on Uncle Mario's and Aunt Ruth's dining room sideboard. It was just an early November get-together, but for the size of the feast they had prepared, it might as well have been Thanksgiving Day.

Vanessa was so hungry that she could imagine the tastes of each dish.

"Come help yourselves, everyone," said Aunt Ruth, plump cheeks pink with heat from the kitchen.

Vanessa hated to be rude. But that was how it would seem if she didn't eat. Aunt Ruth and Uncle Mario were her aunt and uncle now, too—not just Ricki's. Still, she wasn't sure they'd understand that she was a vegetarian. No one else seemed to.

Anita went first in line, tailed closely by Ricki and her little cousins, Anthony and Carlos. As usual, Ricki heaped her plate, helping the kids pile theirs, too.

Vanessa lingered with Gordon and Suzanne on the living room sofa, hoping her father would go in with the others. Maybe he wouldn't notice her.

Wrong.

"Come on, Vee. Chow time." Dad waved to her.

Suzanne and Gordon got up, depriving Vanessa of her excuse to stay behind.

As they neared the dining room, Gordon rubbed his hands together. "Been looking forward to another one of these Mexican feasts ever since your wedding, Andy. Best stuff in town."

Andy nodded. "I couldn't have picked better in-laws, could I, Mario?"

Carrying in a platter of guacamole, Uncle Mario laughed. "Me, neither. Best customers in town."

Vanessa lurked behind Suzanne, doing her best to be inconspicuous.

"Oh, no. You've got that look on your face again," Andy said.

"Me?" Vanessa blinked.

"Yes, you." Her dad shook his head. "Don't tell me you're not going to eat."

A surge of heat rushed to Vanessa's cheeks. Did her dad *have* to start on his favorite subject again, right in front of everyone?

"Aren't you feeling well?" Suzanne laid a hand softly on Vanessa's shoulder.

"How can she be feeling well?" Andy sighed. "She's become a vegetarian."

"Really?" Suzanne's dark eyes grew wide. "You have?"

Vanessa's heart sank. Now Suzanne was harassing her, too, along with Dad.

In line behind them, Aunt Laura jumped into the conversation next. "You're a veg, Vee?"

127

Vanessa just nodded.

Gordon rolled his eyes. "Oh, no. Now we've got another one."

"You make it sound like a disease." Suzanne poked him in the ribs.

"What do you mean, 'another one'?" asked Aunt Laura. "Are you a vegetarian, Suzanne?"

Suzanne nodded. "Twelve years."

"So am I," said Aunt Laura.

Vanessa's eyebrows rose. "You are? Both of you?"

"It was airline food that got me started." Suzanne laughed. "How about you, Laura?"

"The animal dissection assignments in my microbiology classes." Aunt Laura shook her head. "Not a pretty picture."

Vanessa frowned. "I never noticed that you two don't eat meat."

Suzanne interrupted her with a smile. "I don't advertise. Some people have this uncontrollable urge to tease vegetarians." She glared at Gordon.

Aunt Laura nodded. "Fortunately, though, neither of us has a father who pesters us about it or announces it to the *whole universe*." Aunt Laura shoved an elbow at Andy.

"Hey, I'm not pestering Vee. I'm just concerned. Look how pale and thin she is."

"I've always been pale and thin, Dad."

Suzanne laughed again. "That's the popular image of vegetarians. That we're all unfit and hungry."

Vanessa didn't admit that the last half of that description had some merit.

128

"The truth is," said Aunt Laura, "that we get as good as or better nutrition than anyone else. Just have to hit the right food groups."

"Yeah. Carob chip cookies and tofu ice cream, in Suzanne's case." Gordon snickered.

Suzanne made a face at him.

Aunt Laura shrugged. "Being a veg isn't a big deal, Andy. You should know that. You cook healthy. There's just a small step between healthy food and veg food. Vanessa's not going to waste away being a vegetarian."

Suzanne nodded. "Listen, Vanessa. To ease your father's mind, why don't you get him to take you to the doctor for a checkup, and while you're there consult the doctor about a nutrition plan."

"Great idea," Aunt Laura agreed. "See, here's an example of perfectly decent veg nutrition." She pointed at her plate as she helped herself to the buffet. "Corn tortilla, stuffed with pinto beans and rice. Those are complimentary proteins. Add some vegetable side dishes, maybe some fruit, and you're doing pretty well."

"Read up on it, Andy," said Suzanne. "You'll see. It's easy."

"And stop pestering my niece," Aunt Laura added.

"Hmm." Andy grinned and shook his head. "Guess I'm not going to have a chance, am I, with you two riding shotgun for her?"

Gordon leaned over from his spot near the tamales and stage-whispered, "It's a conspiracy. Invasion of the vegetarians."

Together, Suzanne and Aunt Laura gave him a playful shove. Andy laughed along, and just like that, the crisis was over.

Eating spicy beans and savory rice rolled up in a tortilla, topped with a mound of fresh guacamole, Vanessa decided the concoction tasted just like the vegetarian burritos at The Happy Carrot Cafe. Delicious! Why hadn't she thought of it before? She had seconds, which seemed to make her dad happy.

He wandered over and sat next to her, grinning ear to ear. "Hi."

"Hi."

"Good lunch?"

Vanessa nodded.

"Am I pestering you?" he asked, resting his chin on a palm.

Vanessa shrugged.

"I don't mean to. I haven't meant to. I was just worried. I thought you were going along with a fad."

"A fad? You mean vegetarianism?"

Andy nodded. "It's kind of fashionable these days. Rock stars and actors and even English princes . . ."

"Dad, I'm not just going along with a fad." Vanessa frowned.

"I know, Vee." He put his hand on hers. "I wasn't taking you seriously, was I?" A pause. "Listen, I'm open to suggestions. What do you think about that idea of Suzanne's and Laura's—going to visit Dr. Castelli next week? It sounds good to me. And I'll read up on vegetarian nutrition. That is, if you'll promise to do the same. If you're going to do this, I want you to do it right."

Vanessa nodded. "I guess I haven't been doing it right. I mean, I have been kind of hungry sometimes."

"Wouldn't be surprised." Andy shook his head. "Let's not let that happen again, okay?" He gave her a one-armed hug.

"Dad?" Vanessa chewed on her cheek. She wondered if she should push her luck, now that he was finally being understanding. "There's something else I'm not sure if— Well, if you take me seriously about it."

Her dad held her away and looked at her. "Should I guess?"

Vanessa swallowed. "You probably can. The wildlife center. You don't seem to think it's important. At least, not enough for me to spend time there."

"The problem," he answered, "is that you spend too much time there."

Shrugging, Vanessa said, "Maybe I did in the beginning, but even then, my grades never fell. I always got my homework done. I practiced cello."

"And you were wearing yourself out. Too much is too much, Vee."

"But two days, two hours a week is not enough." Vanessa was starting to feel like a whining child. She tried to make herself sound calm and adult. "I really learn a lot at the center, Dad. Maybe I'll be a veterinarian some day or a—"

He sighed. "How much time there would you feel is enough?"

"Well, every day . . ." she began.

131

"How about every other day?"

Something told Vanessa she'd better go for the offer. At least it was an improvement. "All right. It's a deal."

Andy laughed. "Why do I feel like I'm on a used car lot?"

Vanessa shrugged and laughed, too. She felt about ninety-nine percent wonderful. Her dad understood again. And she understood him better, too. He had just been worried about her. But the remaining one percent of her mood had nothing to do with her dad or vegetarian burritos or the wildlife center. That one percent had a funny haircut and gold pierced earrings and at that moment sat across the room. Ricki and Vanessa hadn't really and truly talked in nearly two weeks. Thinking about that fact made Vanessa feel about a hundred percent awful.

Uncle Mario's booming voice startled her. "Christmas!" he was saying. "Our first one all together— one big, noisy family!"

Anita chuckled but shook her head. "Maybe not this Christmas, Mario. Our part of this big, noisy family may have plans to go east."

"East? What's east?"

"Boston, Massachusetts," Andy said. "Vee's grandparents—her mother's parents—live in Boston. Vee and I have migrated back there every year for the holidays with them."

Uncle Mario's face fell. "Oh." He sighed. "Then you'll miss Mom and Pop's fifty-third anniversary party."

"You're kidding," said Ricki. "I didn't know Grandma and Grandpa were having a party."

"A big bash," Aunt Ruth explained. "Didn't your mom tell you?"

Everyone looked at Anita, who shrugged sheepishly. "No, I didn't, because I know the trip east is important, too, so . . ."

"Parties at the farm are always so cool," said Ricki. She glanced at Vanessa. Their eyes met for about half a second, then they both glanced away. That's how it had been since Ricki cut her hair. No yelling or screaming or anything. Just avoiding, politely. So much for the Sisters Team.

As far as her hair went, the rest of the family seemed to have gotten used to it. Or at least, they weren't ribbing her about it anymore. No more light socket jokes from Uncle Mario or rusty axe cracks from Gordon.

Still, Ricki felt as if those scissors of Alison's hadn't just cut off her hair. They had cut a hole out of part of her life—the part where Vanessa used to be.

"What's the date of the anniversary bash?" asked Andy.

Aunt Ruth smoothed back her auburn hair. "December twenty-first. When were you planning on your trip to see Vanessa's grandparents?"

"We usually leave around the nineteenth to be there in time for their rounds of family gatherings," said Andy.

"It's wonderful that you see them every year," said Aunt Laura.

Andy nodded. "They sometimes visit us in the spring or summer. But they're older now, and it's hard for them to travel in the winter."

"Well, if they could," suggested Uncle Mario, "we'd love to have them join us all at the farm." His brown eyes looked hopeful.

That, thought Ricki, was about the closest to pushy that easygoing Uncle Mario ever got.

"I guess we'll have to see how things work out." Andy finally said.

Everyone went quiet. If tension were electricity, Vanessa decided, the room would have been buzzing at that moment. She could tell that Anita and Ricki really wanted Andy to say, "Sure, we'll stay here for the holidays!" So did Uncle Mario and Aunt Ruth and Aunt Laura. But Andy couldn't say that. For one thing, he knew that Vanessa wouldn't trade Christmas with her grandparents for the world. And she knew that he really looked forward to holidays with them, too. Over the years, they had sort of adopted him as a son, although he wasn't even their son-in-law anymore, since he and Mama divorced. Because Andy's own parents were dead, and Mama rarely went home for Christmas, they all needed one another. Nona and Papa needed a son, Andy needed parents, and between them all they shared Vanessa.

She didn't expect Ricki or her side of the family to understand that.

"Well, there's always Thanksgiving," said Aunt Laura brightly, in an obvious effort to break the tension. "Mario, are you and Ruth going to have your annual 'do'?"

"You bet." He nodded.

Anita shook her head. "Guess what, guys? We're already booked for that holiday, too."

"You are?" asked Aunt Ruth.

Gordon spoke up. "I confess. Suzanne and I are the villains. We're stealing them away to my cousin's cottage up in Mendocino."

Blinking, Uncle Mario said, "Oh."

The word was like an iron anchor dragging the conversation to a halt.

On one side of the room, Ricki bit at a thumbnail.

On the other side of the room, Vanessa chewed on her cheek. Something had just occurred to her—a possibility that would make things even more complicated. Mama. In her last letter, she had promised to visit soon.

To Mama, the word "soon," like most words having to do with time and promises, could mean almost anything. What if in this case, it meant the holidays?

"Art," said Mr. Rolph, Ricki's photography teacher, "is a form of self-expression. In that sense, photography is an art, wouldn't you all agree?"

Some of the kids in the circle of desks around his nodded. A couple of them yawned. Mr. Rolph was deep into one of his lectures on the meaning of photography. You either loved them or you hated them. Today, Ricki felt somewhere in between.

"Photography may seem to be a different kind of art, because it employs complicated machines, chemicals, and other sophisticated equipment. At this point in the semester, you are all familiar with the technical aspects of the art.''

Ricki nodded. She already knew how to use a camera and process film and enlarge prints. In fact, she had learned all that with Mrs. McNee at the community center over the summer. The school photography class had so far been mostly a rehash.

''But it also requires the human eye, the human brain, the human heart. The eye, to frame a good shot. The brain, to make the crucial decisions of focus and film speed. And the heart, for that indefinable quality of human involvement.''

Ricki doodled on the cover of her math notebook. Indefinable quality? What did that mean?

''The project I'm assigning,'' said Mr. Rolph, ''is meant to work on that last aspect of photography. Heart and humanity. The project will sound difficult to you at first, I'm sure, but relax. This type of thing has been done many, many times before, with great success. How many of you are familiar with the term 'photo essay'?''

One or two hands went up. Ricki shrugged. She had heard of it, so her hand went up halfway.

''It means just what it sounds like,'' explained Mr. Rolph. ''It's an essay—an expression of a thought, an idea, an opinion, done through photographic images.''

One thing Mr. Rolph was right about. The project definitely sounded hard. By the end of his description of what they were supposed to do, it sounded impossible.

"What subject will your photo essay be on?" Alison asked Ricki in the hall after class.

Ricki shook her head. "I have no earthly idea. I've never been great at even *writing* essays. How am I supposed to do one with just pictures?"

"I don't know either." Alison shrugged. "I'm stumped. Even though it made plenty of sense when he showed us those photo essays by famous photographers. Like the ones by that woman of hungry families during the Great Depression."

"I know," agreed Ricki. "I guess I see photo essays in magazines all the time, but I never knew that's what they were. And I sure never knew I was going to have to do one myself. I have no idea even what to do one on."

Alison nodded. "Oh, well. I guess we'll figure something out."

Walking down the hall to her next class, Ricki tapped a finger on her chin. Mr. Rolph said the subject you pick should be something you are curious about or interested in. Maybe an activities club or a sports team, or how your mother installed a shelf or your father baked a pie. Or it could be on a particular person or even a building or a tree, as long as you were saying something with a set of pictures. None of those options sounded very exciting to Ricki. She had already taken pictures of a sport, cheerleading. She had already done a person, Aunt Allegra, and a building, her house. Over the Thanksgiving holiday, she even did a whole town, Mendocino, the New England-style village where she and her family had

stayed with Suzanne and Gordon. None of those pos-
sibilities seemed very interesting anymore.

But Mr. Rolph had mentioned a third type of subject. He said you could focus on a situation or problem, like what Dorothea Lange did in the 1930s, the
years of the Great Depression. She photographed
families who couldn't find work or even enough food.

Ricki opened her locker. She dumped her science
and photography books in and took her math book
out. In the old days, she could have talked to Vanessa
about something like this. Talking to Vanessa always
helped her get ideas. Not nowadays, though.

In Mendocino, Vanessa had spent practically the
whole weekend talking with Suzanne about vegetarians and animal rights stuff. And after math class that
very day, Ricki had tried to say hi to her, but Vanessa
was so busy talking to Louise Ann, she didn't even
notice. It was as if Vanessa was in another world.

Ricki slammed her locker door shut.

"Vanessa? Is that you?"

"Hi, Anita," Vanessa called as she shut the front
door behind her. "Hi, Kirby!"

The dog came bounding full tilt out through the
dining room to greet her.

"How's my pup?" Vanessa scratched behind his
ears.

As usual, Kirby gave her sneakers a thorough
sniffing to answer all his questions about where she'd
been and what she'd been up to. On Tuesday, Friday,
and Saturday he was always extra interested because

of the smells of squirrels, ducks, and raccoons lingering on her.

"Yes, I've been at Clem's, and I'm beat, and I know you need your walk, but you'll have to wait till after dinner, okay?"

He leaned against her as if to say he'd forgive the delay.

"Vee!" called her dad. "We're in the kitchen."

"Working on a joint project," added Anita.

"Smells good," said Vanessa as she walked in. She lifted a pot lid.

"Ah-ah!" Her dad swatted her hand with an oven mitt. "That's not ready yet. Anyway, it's not the surprise."

"What's the surprise?"

"Can't say." Anita shook her head. "It's a surprise."

"Food," said Andy. "That's a hint."

"Wow." Vanessa peeked under the aluminum foil over a large baking pan and sniffed. "What's this?"

"Oh. The surprise." Anita smiled.

"Courtesy of Aunt Laura," Andy said. "She gave us the recipe."

"Vegetarian pizza," said Anita, as proudly as if they had just invented the wheel.

"Wow!" Vanessa clapped her hands. "For me?"

Anita laughed. "Well, you'll have to share. We've decided it wouldn't hurt all of us to take in a little less meat and focus more on vegetables."

Steam from the pots on the stove rose up around Anita's face, making her cheeks glow. Her dad looked rosy and happy, too.

Things had been going much better recently. The

doctor and a couple of books had assured her dad that a vegetarian diet wouldn't turn Vanessa into a walking carrot. He no longer hovered over her at meals. Vanessa, on the other hand, didn't go hungry anymore.

She took a fork from the drawer and tore off a bite of the pizza. "Mmm!" Then she snitched pieces of the cucumber Anita was slicing into a salad.

"Ricki better get home soon," Andy said, "or we won't have any dinner left."

Anita glanced at the giraffe clock. "She's due back at six-thirty. The soccer team is having a Thanksgiving leftovers party."

"Hey, that's where we should be. I'm in the mood for a holiday party."

Anita sighed. "Me, too. Speaking of which, we've got some news on our holiday plans, Vanessa."

"Good or bad?" Vanessa asked, filching another cucumber slice.

Andy laughed. "You decide. Ever hear the saying, 'Compromise is the finest of arts'?"

"Now I have."

"Well, that's what we're going to do," said her dad. "Compromise."

"In other words, we're going to do *everything* over the holidays," explained Anita.

"Does that mean we're still going to Boston to see Papa and Nona?" asked Vanessa.

Anita nodded. "Absolutely. *And* we're going to my folks' anniversary party before Boston, then we'll be back in time to throw a New Year's Eve party of our own here."

"Oh," said Vanessa. "I guess that means we'll spend less time with Nona and Papa than usual, doesn't it?"

Anita nodded again. "I'm afraid so. To work everything in, like your dad said, we have to compromise. Are you disappointed?"

Vanessa shrugged. "A little. But I *was* afraid we wouldn't get to go at all."

"What we're doing," said Andy, "is trying to please everyone and do everything, which is exactly what advice columnists tell you not to do."

"Holidays are such a hectic time," said Anita. "The most sensible thing is to do what's most convenient."

"And of course we're doing exactly the opposite." her dad smiled brightly. "We're planning the least convenient, most hectic holidays ever, rushing back and forth across the country, across the state. . . ."

Vanessa giggled. "Sounds like fun."

"We had a feeling you girls would say that." Anita winked.

Helping Anita peel carrots, Vanessa's thoughts wandered to Christmas. This year would be their first together as a family. Last year, the idea of holidays all together had been only a dream. Now, she and Ricki had exactly what they wanted. Almost. The family was together, but what about the two of them? Maybe they had become real sisters now—taking each other for granted, living separate lives, with separate friends and separate viewpoints. . . .

"I chatted with Dr. Rosen out by the mailboxes today," her dad was saying.

"Poor guy. He always looks so . . ." Anita's voice trailed off.

"Lonesome?" he nodded. "Yeah. I was thinking we ought to have him over more often. Anyway, today we talked about the neighborhood."

"What about it?" asked Vanessa.

"Well, you'll be very interested in this, Vee. And I'm sure I'll have to repeat every word when Ricki gets home. Dr. Rosen made a confession. Get this. He and your Clementine Hewitt were childhood sweethearts."

"You must be joking!" Vanessa's eyebrows rose. "She always calls him 'that milquetoast sap.' "

Dad chuckled. "It seems Emmett the sailor once beat Dr. Rosen in an arm wrestling match out on our front porch. Clem still held out for Dr. Rosen, though. And get this . . . she even got engaged to him just before Emmett drowned in that shipwreck."

"Really, Andy?" Anita's dark eyes grew huge.

"That's what the man said. But apparently her parents forced them to break off the engagement, and she never forgave him for allowing them to drive him away."

"Wow," Vanessa whispered. "This is just like 'Day After Day.' "

"Like what?" asked Anita.

"I believe it's a soap opera," Andy translated. "Anyway . . . Oh, wait. Was that the doorbell?"

"Good." Anita wiped her hands on a dish towel. "It must be Ricki. We can eat now. She must have forgotten her keys again."

142

Vanessa was already dashing toward the hall. "I'll get it!"

She had made a decision. It was time for one of them to take the first step. Either she or Ricki had to act maturely and responsibly and try to straighten things out between them.

The bell rang again.

It had to be Ricki. Who else would be impatient enough to ring twice in twenty seconds?

"All right, all right, Ricki. I'm coming." Unlocking the dead bolt, Vanessa heard a voice on the other side say, "It's not Ricki."

"It's not?" Vanessa whispered, peeking through the peephole.

She saw a petite, slender woman in a gold brocade jacket and skirt. The woman wore pearl earrings, a pearl necklace, and a small white hat with one long gold feather.

As if in a dream, Vanessa turned the doorknob. She opened the door murmuring, "Mama?"

Chapter 13

Within half a second, Vanessa was enveloped by silk and the sweet fragrance of roses. Mama's touch, Mama's scent.

"Oh, darling, darling. I've missed you!" Mama's voice, like honey.

For a moment, Vanessa couldn't move. She still felt as if she were dreaming. Then Mama's small, light hand was on her shoulder. "Let me look at you."

They stood for a moment together. The first thing Vanessa realized was that she was nearly as tall as her mother. They stood almost eye to eye. The last time they'd been together—two Easters ago—Vanessa had had to look up at Mama.

The next thing she noticed was eerie. The longer she looked at Mama, the more she felt she was looking into a mirror. They shared the same shade of vanilla blond hair. The same shade of forest green eyes. And the same pointy, pouty chin.

"Your grandmother has been sending me photographs of you, darling. But nothing prepared me for this. You're my double!" Mama's smile sparkled.

Vanessa nodded. "That's just what I was thinking."

Mama embraced her again. "Oh, darling Vanessa."

In the middle of the hug, Vanessa felt her mother's body suddenly stiffen.

"Hello, Celeste." Andy's voice came from behind them.

Vanessa turned to find him and Anita standing together in the entry.

"Well, hello, Andy. And you must be Anita." Mama took a step forward and held out her hand.

Anita took it. "Pleasure to meet you, Celeste." She smiled.

Mama smiled back. "Well, I must apologize for dropping in on you this way. I know it's terribly rude, but—"

"No, it's not, Mama," Vanessa said. "I'm glad you're here!"

"Of course, it's fine," said Anita.

"Come on in, Celeste." Andy waved her in.

Mama slipped her hat off. She fiddled with the feather. "Thank you. I just flew in from the islands this morning. On the—what do they call those things? Red eye? Up all night. I must look terrible."

"You're beautiful!" said Vanessa, taking Mama's hand.

This was all completely different from what Vanessa had expected. She had thought that she would be a nervous wreck when Mama finally came to see her. Tongue-tied, shy, not knowing how to act or what to say. After all, it had been over a year and a half since she'd seen her mother.

But now that Mama was really there, her worries

145

floated away. All she felt was happy. Super, fantastically happy!

Andy and Anita ushered Mama into the living room. Right away they sent Vanessa into the kitchen for tea.

Vanessa knew what that was for—to give them a chance to talk out the grown-up details of her mother's visit. When her dad and Mama divorced, they didn't set up official custody or visitation rights for Vanessa. They just worked it out as they went along. And because Mama only came around once a year or so, the subject hardly ever came up.

Vanessa didn't worry about it. Her dad always let Mama see her as much as she wanted.

When she finally walked back into the living room carrying a tray of cups and the teapot, Anita was inviting Celeste to stay for dinner.

"Oh." Mama shook her head. "Thank you. I couldn't impose. I'll just come by tomorrow and—"

"Oh, please, Mama, stay." Vanessa pleaded.

"Well . . ."

Just then Ricki burst in through the front door. "Hi, everybody! I'm home! What's for dinner?"

Mama laughed softly. "You must be Ricki."

Andy made the introductions, and after that, everything seemed to pass in a blur. Mama stayed for dinner. She told them about living on Oahu and the volcano that erupted on one of the other Hawaiian islands and then about Canada, where she had lived before Hawaii. But it seemed that Vanessa had barely had a chance to blink before dinner was over, and just a little while later her mother was saying she must go.

With a promise to take Vanessa out to dinner tomorrow, Mama gave her a good-night kiss and was gone.

One more math problem.

That was it, then Ricki could put on a Talking Heads tape and relax.

Math didn't seem so scary anymore. No longer was she terrified of being called to the board by Mrs. Minsk. Ricki never had gotten revenge on Schuyler for snickering at her that day, but at least now he wouldn't have another chance.

These days, Ricki's only school trouble was photography, of all things. For the life of her, she couldn't figure out what to do her photo essay on. Her brain just wouldn't get going on ideas.

She tapped her pencil on the desk. Lately, nothing came easily. Not even friendship. It was so complicated. Vanessa lived on a cloud now that Celeste was around. Last night at dinner, the rest of the world may as well have been vaporized by Martians, for all Vanessa cared.

Ricki sighed.

She put her name in the upper right-hand corner of her homework sheet, slipped it into her binder, then hurried to her stereo. That's what she needed. A little music to pep her up.

She was just about to push the cassette in when the doorbell rang. Next came Andy's footsteps in the entry, the front door opening, and voices.

"Hi, Celeste."

"Hello, Andy. I'm early, aren't I?"

"Yup. It's okay. Vanessa's getting dressed. Come on into the living room. I'll tell her you're here."

Ah-hah! So that was why Vanessa had been in the bathroom for the last hour, thought Ricki. She was going out with her mother.

Ricki heard the bathroom door open.

"Hi, Mama!" Vanessa called downstairs.

Laying the tape on top of the stereo, Ricki bunched her mouth to the side. *What would it hurt?* she asked herself. She walked slowly down the hall to Vanessa's room.

"Hi," she said, standing in the doorway.

Vanessa was hidden by a green turtleneck sweater she had managed to pull only halfway over her head. A muffled "hi" came from under it.

"Need help?" asked Ricki.

Vanessa finally pulled the sweater down. "Got it." She barely glanced at Ricki.

"Well . . ." Ricki shuffled her feet. "I just wanted to say, have a good time with your mom."

Examining herself in the mirror, Vanessa nodded. "Oh, thanks." She brushed her hair with hurried strokes.

"Sure," said Ricki. "You're welcome." Cookies. Cookies and some good music. That was what she needed. She started downstairs. About halfway, she heard Celeste's high, tinkling laugh, a sound like wind chimes. Andy said something and chuckled.

Ricki shook her head. It was really weird how divorced people acted around each other. How could they be so polite—even friendly—after having split up a marriage? She shrugged and was about to go on to the kitchen when she heard Celeste's pretty voice again.

"We had some lovely times together, didn't we, Andy?"

For a while, he didn't answer. Then he said, "Yes, we did." In his voice, there was something funny. It was like a scene in a movie, when two people are stuck in an elevator together, and the air is running out, and they start saying really deep things.

"You've done a tremendous job with Vanessa," said Celeste. "She seems happy."

"She is, I think," Andy answered. "And she's very happy to see you, Celeste. You mean a great deal to her."

"Oh. Thank you. I appreciate your saying that."

"I'm not just saying that," Andy insisted. "It's true."

Another patch of silence.

"I'd like to see her more often. I can't." The voice was no longer clear and pretty. It turned cloudy. "I simply can't come more often. I wish—I wish things could be different."

Ricki rolled her eyes. "Give me a break," she whispered. This was disgusting. Why *couldn't* Celeste come more often to see her daughter? What kind of mom was she, anyway? At least she didn't have to whine about it.

Seeing Vanessa's photos of her mother, Ricki used to think Celeste was cool and glamorous. She had been really impressed. But now she hardly even liked

Vanessa's mom. Last night at dinner all Celeste talked about was herself. Sure, it was interesting to hear about all the places she'd traveled to and what it was like being on stage and all, but Celeste seemed to be on stage *all the time*.

"Well," she was saying, "it's so nice to see you again, Andy. You're looking wonderful."

Ricki's eyes narrowed. Celeste's voice had changed again. Now it was smooth and silky, like someone who was dreaming. Or flirting. That was it!

A hard, hot blush drove up along Ricki's throat to her face. Celeste was flirting with Andy!

"Excuse me."

Ricki jumped. Charging past her down the stairs came Vanessa and Kirby.

"See you later." Vanessa waved.

"Right," said Ricki. "Later."

Ricki watched as Vanessa rushed into the living room and flew into her mother's arms.

"Lovely!" cried Celeste. "Is my lovely little bird ready for a night on the town? We're going to the Carnelian Room in San Francisco, Andy, and don't expect us home until ten. Is that all right?"

"That's fine. Have fun."

Celeste answered with a tinkly laugh, and then, "How could I not, with such a charming young companion?"

Ricki thought she was going to be sick.

Vanessa's arms ached. Carrying two big shopping bags all around Union Square in San Francisco Thursday afternoon had been hard work. Shopping with Mama was very different from shopping with her dad.

"I can't believe all these clothes, Mama!" Vanessa heaved the bags out of the trunk of her mother's rented car in the driveway at home. "Thanks again!"

"Do you realize," asked her mother, smiling, "that is the sixth time you've thanked me?" She smoothed Vanessa's bangs, then took one of the bags to carry up the path.

Vanessa giggled. "I can't help it. I've never had so many new clothes in my life!"

"You're growing," said her mother. "And growing *up*. You'll be needing nice things."

"You really didn't have to, Mama. I mean—"

Her mother put a mauve-painted fingernail to her lips. "Shh. Not another word about it. We had fun, didn't we?" She winked and laughed.

At the front door, Vanessa set the shopping bag down to take her house keys from her purse. As she unlocked the door, her mother handed her the shopping bag she had been carrying.

"Here," she said.

Taking it, Vanessa noticed an odd look on her mother's face. "What's wrong?"

Her mother smiled. "Darling, I'm not coming in with you."

"Oh. You have to get back to the hotel?"

She shook her head. "I have to go to the airport."

"The airport?"

"Sorry, darling. I have to leave tonight. I've been offered a holiday booking at the Palm Court in Miami, and I have to take it."

"Oh." Vanessa dropped the shopping bag and studied the porch floorboards beside it.

"I knew you'd understand." With her fingers, Mama gently lifted Vanessa's chin. "You're my treasure, darling. Do you know that?"

Vanessa couldn't answer. Her eyes stayed focused on the porch floor, brimming with tears.

"You'll always be my little girl," Mama whispered, then sighed. "I can't—I haven't been much of a mother for you these last years. But you do remember some of our old times together, don't you?"

Vanessa nodded slowly.

"I'm glad, darling. And listen. Things are about to change for me. After the holidays in Florida, I'm going to New York. Someone I know is putting together an off-Broadway show, and I just may get the singing lead. Wouldn't that be something? And after that, I think I'd like to stay put. Set up a voice studio, try teaching. New York wouldn't be a bad place to come visit me, would it?"

Vanessa looked up. "You really think you might stay there?"

"I'm working on it, love. Doing my best." Mama pulled a rose-scented handkerchief from her purse and dried Vanessa's tears.

Her own eyes had begun to glisten. "Now, I really have to go. Can't miss that plane." She cupped Vanessa's face in her small, soft hands. "All right?"

Slowly, Vanessa nodded.

She wrapped her arms around her mother. Then she let go. "Good-bye."

"Good-bye, darling."

Mama walked away.

Vanessa went inside and didn't look back. She left the shopping bags on the porch.

Ricki yawned. Boy, had it been a long day! A science test, a soccer game, and tons of homework. She could barely keep her eyes open long enough to brush her teeth.

Leaving the bathroom, all she could think of was crawling into bed. Then she nearly tripped on something—a paw.

"Kirby?" She shook her head at the dog stretched out in the hall. "What are you trying to do—break my neck?"

He whined. His chin lay on his paws, lining his nose right up to the threshold of Vanessa's bedroom door.

Ricki frowned. No light shone under the door. Vanessa must have gone to bed early and forgotten to let her dog in. She had seemed pretty quiet at dinner, probably because her precious mother was gone.

That Celeste. Weird person. One day flirting with her ex-husband, the next day taking off.

Ricki still felt annoyed. She wondered if she should tell her mom about the flirting, then quickly decided against it. The whole thing had been pretty mild and completely one-sided. It wasn't as if Andy flirted back or anything!

Anyway, she and Vanessa had promised each other

not to interfere in their parents' marriage. In the past, the two of them would have gotten together to talk about something like this. But *this* wasn't exactly the kind of problem to talk over with Vanessa, whose own mother was the problem!

Vanessa seemed to think her mother was some sort of goddess. She worshipped the ground Celeste walked on.

Ricki sighed and headed for her room.

Kirby whined again. He turned his big brown eyes up to Ricki.

"Hey, I know, Kirb. You're locked out, huh?"

He whined again.

"Sorry about that, pal." Ricki paused. "I guess you could *maybe* stay in my room tonight. Maybe. That is, if you promise to be really, really—"

Kirby wasn't paying attention. He sniffed at the threshold of Vanessa's door, pawed at it a couple of times, and whined again.

"Oh. Not interested in any offers from me, huh?" Ricki sighed again. "Okay, you big rug. Let's see if I can get you in there. I don't want you out here blubbering all night." She approached Vanessa's door and quietly turned the knob. Good. It was unlocked.

Kirby jumped to his feet as Ricki slowly opened the door for him.

"Keep him out!" called a voice from the other side.

"Vee?" Ricki peered through the darkness. "He's been out here—"

"I know." Vanessa's voice was so low Ricki could

barely hear her. "I don't want him in my room now, all right?"

"He doesn't like it out here. How come you—"

A long, loud sniffle interrupted Ricki. "I just don't! I don't want him to—" Vanessa couldn't go on. Her voice drowned in a flood of tears.

Chapter 14

"Vee? What's wrong?" Ricki moved through Vanessa's dark room toward the bed. She felt Kirby's warm bulk beside her. Then he went forward. As Ricki's eyes adjusted, she saw him put his paws up on the bed, right in Vanessa's lap. He whimpered softly.

"This . . . is why," Vanessa said, sobbing. "I didn't want him to see me like this. He doesn't understand."

"You mean, he doesn't understand why you're crying?" Ricki asked quietly. "Neither do I. Why are you crying?"

"Oh, you wouldn't understand!" Vanessa wailed. She buried her face in the pillow she held.

Kirby pawed at it.

"Do you mind if we stay for a while?" Ricki asked. "I mean, can I sit down?"

Vanessa, hidden by the pillow, didn't answer.

Ricki sat on the edge of the bed. She bit at a thumbnail. Maybe Celeste wasn't a totally horrible person, if Vanessa missed her this much.

"Your mom?" Ricki asked in a super-soft voice.

The pillow still didn't answer, but Ricki thought she saw it moving up and down in a sort of a nod.

"Why did your mom have to leave so soon, Vee?"

The sound from the pillow was a long, deep moan. It made Ricki's heart ache. She touched her sister's shoulder. "Hey . . ."

Another moan, this one broken by hiccupy sobs.

Ricki put an arm around Vanessa, the pillow, and something big and furry, which turned out to be Kirby's head. Her elbow got a wet slurp from him.

"Thanks," she muttered, then finished hugging her sister.

The pillow finally dropped away.

"I'm not—not interesting," said Vanessa.

"You're not what?" Ricki blinked.

"I'm boring. Dull." Vanessa's voice was still soggy, but now it had a sharp edge to it. "How interesting can I be? A twelve-year-old kid who plays the cello and hangs out with an old woman and squirrels."

"Vee, what are you talking about?"

"Me, Ricki. I'm talking about *me*. You asked why my mother left so soon." Another sob. Then, so quietly that Ricki barely heard it, Vanessa said, "*I'm* why."

"Huh? You mean you think Celeste left because she got bored?"

Vanessa nodded.

"But she's your *mom*, Vee. She loves you."

"I know she does." Vanessa's voice sounded a little calmer. "I know she loves me. I've always known. No matter how much Mama stays away—I know it's not because she doesn't love me. But I—I also know that she can't stay with me. She's restless and always needs to—to be—"

"On stage?" Ricki asked.

"Yes," whispered Vanessa. "I'm not enough for her." A long, deep sob.

"Oh, Vee . . ."

"Sometimes I think that if only I was more . . . I don't know. Maybe more like her. Beautiful and outgoing and charming, with a voice—"

"Oh, come on." Ricki shook her head. "You've got to be kidding. You don't want to be like *her*."

Vanessa sniffled. "Why not?"

Biting her lip, Ricki thought carefully before she answered. She didn't want to be insulting. "Well, for one thing, what's wrong with being *you*?"

"I'm boring."

Ricki rolled her eyes. "Not that again."

"Isn't it true?" Vanessa demanded. "Then how come—how come even *you* don't want to be with me?"

"Huh?"

Vanessa sniffed up a tear, hard. "To you, every kid at Roosevelt is more interesting than me. Dale, Inez, Alison . . ."

"They're my friends, Vee."

"I know. And I'm not anymore."

"What are you talking about?" Ricki sat upright. "You're the one who won't have anything to do with us. All you want to do is hang out with our old friends from intermediate school. And . . . shoot! When you're with Louise Ann, especially when the

158

two of you are yakking about music stuff, I may as
well have dropped off the face of the earth!''

"What? That's ridiculous. You're the one who
ignores *me*."

Ricki shook her head. "You act more stuck-up
than Courtney Haines. You barely even talk to Alison
or Marsha or anyone else when I'm with them, much
less hang out with us.''

"I never knew you wanted me to." Vanessa's
voice was small and pouty.

"I've *asked* you to a million times, Vee."

"So? That was just being polite."

"Oh. I see." Ricki crossed her arms. "You can
read my mind, huh? You've decided that I was just
being polite. You've decided that I think you're boring. Even that your own mother thinks you're boring!
Get off it, Vee. Get real.'' She huffed a breath.

Vanessa's chin jutted out. "How am I supposed to
get real or make any sense out of you, when you
go through a million different personalities in one
semester? First you're a cheerleader pal, then you're
Mucha—"

"Macha," Ricki corrected.

"Whatever. Who knows what'll be next!''

Ricki's arms stayed crossed. Her eyebrows and lips
worked on a heavy scowl. Meanwhile, though, she
was thinking, drumming her fingers on her arm. Had
she really gone through different personalities? Well,
maybe Vanessa had a kind of a point. A small one.
"Are you trying to say I confused you?"

"That," said Vanessa, "is the understatement of

159

the year. We are turning into ordinary, run-of-the-mill sisters. The kind who just live in the same house, share the same parents and the same tube of toothpaste.''

"We *are* sisters," said Ricki.

"But we weren't supposed to be ordinary sisters. That wasn't the plan.''

"I know.'' Ricki shrugged. "So . . . let's not.''

Vanessa looked at Ricki in the dim light. There were Ricki's bright black eyes and her grin. For the first time in weeks, she felt she was truly seeing Ricki. Even with that weird Machas earring and the weirder haircut, even though Ricki had a zillion other friends who were nothing at all like Vanessa, underneath it all there was still Ricki. The real Ricki. Vanessa's sister and best friend. She had been there the whole time.

"Hold it," said Ricki. "Right there. Don't move.''

"Like this?'' Vanessa leaned against the post of a large raccoon pen, arms crossed.

Inside the pen, crouching on the concrete floor, a large, fluffy gray raccoon watched their every move with wide, bandit-masked eyes.

"Perfect,'' declared Ricki, aiming her camera to take in the whole scene. "Wait. Let me get one more.''

"Hurry up. We're not supposed to hang around him too much. He needs to be scared of humans.''

Ricki clicked a last shot, then moved the camera away from her eye. "So you and your family were the ones who scared the daylights out of us, huh?''

She wagged a finger at the raccoon. "Naughty, naughty."

"Can you believe it?" Vanessa said as they walked away from the pen. "Just a couple of months ago he was a cute little kit who fit in the palm of my hand. He had tiny paws and always tried to hold his doll bottle when we fed him. Now Clem says he'll be ready for release in about a month."

From a distance, Ricki clicked another shot of the raccoon pen, then started on the duck pond. Vanessa watched as Ricki followed a brown hen's clumsy waddle around the edge.

At the door of the supply shed a few feet away, Clem held a blue jay in one hand and scooped wild birdseed out of a barrel with the other. So far, she hadn't muttered more than "hello" to the girls. But every once in a while Vanessa caught her glancing at them out of the corner of her eye.

Convincing Clem to let Ricki visit hadn't been as hard as Vanessa had expected it to be. Actually, it had been harder work trying to convince Ricki to come. Monday night the two of them had promised to find out more about each other's new interests. Not to become just ordinary sisters, but to keep on being best friends, too. They didn't have to act like twins, or "clones," as Ricki put it. But it would be nice for each to see what the other had been up to.

This afternoon was part of that plan. Ricki had come to see the wildlife center. In return, Vanessa promised to have lunch with Ricki and her new friends at least one day next week.

"Hey, what's wrong with this guy?" Ricki pointed to a big white goose.

"Don't bother him!" a voice boomed from the shed. "He needs peace and quiet!"

Vanessa was about to reassure Clem that no harm would come to the broken-winged goose, when Ricki suddenly turned her camera on the old woman and snapped the shutter.

Vanessa's heart stopped.

Clem's red lips twisted. Her eyes narrowed. "Did you just take a picture of me, young lady?"

Ricki nodded, keeping the camera to her eye, and snapped again.

"You don't have my permission for that!" Clem snarled.

"Oh," said Ricki from behind the lens. "Why not?"

"Because I said so. No more photographs of me, understand?" Clem whirled around and went back to the birdseed.

"But you look so . . . you know . . . interesting," Ricki called to her. "I mean, with the pretty bird in your hand and everything. It makes a great shot."

Vanessa held her breath. She knew that Ricki's photographer sweet talk would be wasted on Clem. Ricki was playing with fire.

"This isn't a *National Geographic* special," said Clem, "and I'm not Jane Goodall. So cut it out."

"Just one more shot?" Ricki begged.

"Ricki . . ." whispered Vanessa.

From the shed, Clem shot Ricki a look that could melt steel.

Ricki dropped the lens from her eye and shrugged. "Oh, well."

"Come over here, Ricki," said Vanessa, pulling her arm. "Let me show you the squirrels."

Once they were out of Clem's earshot, Ricki grumbled, "Boy, is she a grump! How do you put up with her?"

"Most of the time she's okay," Vanessa explained. "Actually, Clem's very interesting. She knows a lot, and she teaches me."

Ricki shrugged. "Yeah, I guess she must know a lot to take care of all these guys." She panned her camera around, looking for another shot.

"Don't forget she knows how to get them ready to go free in the wild, too," added Vanessa.

"Yeah, that's really cool." Ricki clicked her camera at a cute brown squirrel shelling a peanut with his paws. "Remember over the summer when we found those love letters from Clem's old boyfriend, and we tried to find her through the phone book and everything? Little did we know that here she was, right down the street. Wildlife Woman!"

"Former fiancée of Dr. Rosen!" Vanessa whispered.

"*That's* wild, for sure. Can you believe it?" Ricki shook her head.

"I think she's been reading the letters," Vanessa whispered.

"Really? Good. At least *somebody* gets to read them. How do you know?"

"Oh, just a feeling. One day I went into the house to ask her something and caught her fiddling with some papers at her desk. She stuffed them into a drawer when she saw me. Other times she acts funny. Kind of distracted or dreamy.''

"Clem, dreamy?'' Ricki gave her a sideways look.

Vanessa shrugged. "Well, dreamy for Clem.''

"Wonder if she ever dreams about old Doc Rosen. I can't get over it. Clemmie and Lenny. What a match.''

Vanessa giggled. "Wildlife Woman and Slow-Motion Man.''

Ricki giggled, too. For a few minutes, neither one could stop. It was definitely like old times again. A real, live giggling fit.

When it was over, Vanessa sighed. "Well, you know, the sad thing is that Clem may not be Wildlife Woman for long.''

"Huh?'' Ricki scrunched up her nose. "Oh, you mean because of the money problems you talked about?''

Vanessa nodded. "I don't think it's as hopeless as Clem makes it sound, though. I mean, if only I could convince her to go out and talk to people again the way she used to. She used to go to county government meetings, charity fundraisers, and all that sort of thing.''

"Hah! Good luck. Get the hermit crab to leave her hole? That would be tough. Hey, how about if I enlarge those shots of her really big and give them to her, just for grins?'' Ricki laughed at the thought.

"Sure,'' said Vanessa. "Make her day.''

Ricki laughed again. "Well, I am going to enlarge some of the shots I took here. I got a lot of good ones.

164

Like the raccoon and that sad-looking goose . . ." Her voice trailed off. Something had just occurred to her. "Hey," she whispered. "My project!"

"Which project?"

"My photo essay for photography class," Ricki explained. "This is it! I'm supposed to show something about an important subject."

"You mean, you could do your project about . . . us?" Vanessa had one eyebrow up.

"Yeah, to show all the work you and Clem do, and how you help animals, and— What's wrong?"

"Wrong? The only thing wrong is that I didn't have you visit here sooner! Ricki, after you make this photo essay, could you loan it to me?"

"Well, sure, but— Oh, I get it! You could show it around, right? Like, to the Service Club? Try to get them interested again?"

Vanessa nodded, staring off into the trees. "For starters. Maybe we can't get Clem out in person yet, but we sure can spread information about her and the center, can't we? You're right—you did get some great pictures today." She giggled and slapped Ricki's outstretched palm in a high five. "What a team!"

Chapter 15

Ricki bit at a thumbnail. Five of her photographs of the wildlife center hung on the wall of the school student lounge. The officers of the Roosevelt Junior High Service Club sat in session around a table at the front of the room, gazing at her pictures.

"I think the officers are impressed," whispered Louise Ann from the chair next to her.

"How can you tell?" Vanessa whispered on Ricki's other side.

"Dani said that the first time she tried to tell them about the center, they hardly even paid attention. Now they're paying attention. See, look at Kevin Fong pointing at the raccoon picture. He's the club president, you know."

"Hi," someone whispered from behind Ricki.

Ricki turned and saw the flash of braces over her shoulder. "Got here as soon as I could." It was Kimberly. "Have they voted yet?"

"Not yet," answered Louise Ann. "Dani just made her presentation about the center to them and explained what each picture is about."

At the table beside the officers sat Dani, looking calm and cool.

"But, hey," Louise Ann went on, "I'm shocked you could take time out from your busy schedule, Kimberly, to come show support for your old pals."

Kimberly gave her a little shove. "Oh, Louise Ann, stop giving me a hard time. You didn't tell me about this till two hours ago, remember? I had to wriggle my way out of practice early to get here."

"Yes, you had to tear yourself away from your fellow cheerleaders," said Louise Ann with a mock sigh. "Glad you came."

"Me, too," put in Vanessa. "Thanks, Kimberly. Every face out here counts, to convince the club officers to vote yes."

Kimberly took a seat beside them.

Vanessa felt surprisingly calm. She had thought she'd be a nervous wreck at the meeting, but now, with her best friends all around her, it wasn't so bad. Louise Ann, Kimberly, Dani, and, of course, Ricki. They were working together, as a team.

It almost didn't matter how the club voted, Vanessa decided. If the presentation didn't work here, she'd try it somewhere else. Maybe even City Hall! But a "yes" vote today would definitely be a step in the right direction.

"Well, I think we're ready to decide now, aren't we?" Kevin Fong asked his fellow officers.

Nods around the table.

Kevin cleared his throat, adjusted his big black-framed glasses, and continued. "We've heard Dani's presentation and seen Ricki Romero's photographs. We've also read the description of the center's work that Vanessa Shepherd submitted. It's all very interesting. Thank you all for your time. I think we've gotten a very different view of this project than we had a few weeks ago."

Ricki closed her eyes and crossed her fingers.

Vanessa held her breath.

"All those in favor of adding Clementine Hewitt's wildlife rehabilitation center to the Service Club's list of projects, please say, 'ay.' "

Ricki crossed her fingers tighter.

"Ay!" rang out in a loud, many-voiced chorus.

"Any opposed?" asked Kevin.

There was silence until a loud shout filled the room. "Way . . . to . . . go-o-o-o!" yelled Kimberly, flying into the aisle with a midair split.

Kevin frowned, but all the rest of the club officers and members laughed.

"Looks like we've made a popular decision!" Dani pointed out, giggling.

Vanessa and Ricki grinned at each other.

"She *has* to come," said Vanessa, frowning at her watch. "She promised."

Ricki shook her head. "I told you, getting Clementine Hewitt out of her house would be like prying a hermit crab from a hole."

"But she even looked a little excited. I mean, as excited as Clem gets. She didn't exactly jump up and down, but she didn't grump at me, either. Then your mother personally went down and invited her. I think that did the trick."

"Hah! Clementine, excited about a New Year's Eve party? Tell me another joke. It would be like

Scrooge at Christmas." Ricki poured herself another cup of pineapple punch, careful not to spill it on her new red velvet jumpsuit, a Christmas present from her grandparents. She and Vanessa were both dressed to the nines, as assistant hosts for their parents' party.

"Oh, Ricki. You just don't know Clem Hewitt. She's got a tough shell, but underneath she's a softie. You should have seen the look on her face when I told her about the Service Club taking the wildlife center on as a project."

"She growled and snarled?"

"Not a bit. I'm not positive, but I think I saw a tear in her eye. I mean, it seemed to mean a lot to her that someone cares about what she's doing." Vanessa leaned her head to the side. Her long, brush-sheened hair fell over the shoulder of her green dress—one of the Union Square things Mama had gotten her. "I think Clem is really just lonely for company. That's why she puts up the grumpy front— so no one will know just how alone she is."

"*Human* company, you mean. She's got plenty of other kinds."

Vanessa smiled. "That's for sure."

"Hey, speaking of being lonely for company, look who's over on the sofa."

"Dr. Rosen. Well, he's not *all* alone. Kirby's sitting beside him," Vanessa noted.

"The dog is fascinated. He probably never met anyone so quiet."

"At least not in *our* family." Vanessa shook her head. "Poor Dr. Rosen."

"Slow-Motion Man," said Ricki. "Dr. Slo Mo.

Can you imagine, him and Clementine, fiancés? Wow. Two more opposite kinds of people I never met."

"Hmm." Vanessa raised an eyebrow. "Are you sure about that?"

"Oh. Well, *almost* never met." Ricki bunched her mouth to the side. "There were these two other people."

"Who actually ended up married," Vanessa pointed out.

The girls gazed across the living room at their parents. Tall, slender Anita, in a glittery silver holiday dress, stood beside shorter, stockier Andy, in his old faded jeans and a red bow tie for the occasion. They held their arms lightly around each other's waists.

"They're different, all right," said Vanessa.

Ricki nodded. "And you and I should know about differences."

"Which make for good teams, right? Remember that old theory?" Vanessa asked. "Opposites attract?"

"Well, you have to have *some* things in common. For instance—"

The chime of the doorbell interrupted Ricki. She and Vanessa watched as Andy let in a woman bundled in a black overcoat. Then the woman took it off, revealing a lacy, white blouse and long yellow skirt.

"Oh, my gosh!" gasped Vanessa.

"Holy kazoo!" added Ricki.

"It's her!"

"She's actually looks . . . *human* tonight."

"No gray sack dress," whispered Vanessa. "I didn't know Clem even owned anything else."

"No scary red lipstick," Ricki said. "And she combed her hair."

"First time this week, probably. I need to go over and welcome her."

"Vee, wait." Ricki grabbed her sister's arm.

"What?"

"Well, I was just thinking. You know that theory? Opposites attract?"

Vanessa nodded. "Yes?"

"And differences make for good teams?" Ricki grinned. "Well, isn't it kind of sad that, after all these years, Clementine and Dr. Rosen—"

Vanessa's left eyebrow rose. "Ricki, you're not thinking . . ."

The girls' eyes swiveled to Dr. Rosen. He sat absolutely still on the sofa beside Kirby. His eyes were focused on the entryway. His jaw hung open.

"He looks like he's in shock," said Ricki.

"Or like he's seeing a ghost." Vanessa chewed on her cheek. "A ghost from his past. Ricki, what if they hate each other?"

Ricki shrugged. "Well, remember Mom and Andy? They didn't exactly get along at first."

Vanessa smiled. "We did accomplish quite a feat getting *them* together."

"The Sisters Scheme." Ricki tapped a finger on her chin. "We didn't do too badly."

"Are you telling me you're ready to try it again?" Vanessa leaned closer to her sister and whispered.

171

"Are *you*?" asked Ricki.

Vanessa winked at her sister. "It's always fun to try old theories."

Ricki winked back. "Look out. The Sisters Team is on the way!"